Jordan leaned in close. "You okay?"

Brady slowly turned his head to look Jordan in the eye. "I'm good. And I like Belinda. Drake, on the other hand, seemed a little surprised to see me."

Jordan sighed. "Which means at some point this evening, he'll corner me, dying to know more." His hand was still resting against Brady's back, and the intimacy of his stance set up a fluttering in Brady's belly.

Before he could give himself time to change his mind, Brady shifted even closer and whispered, "Want to really give him something to talk about?" He cupped Jordan's cheek and moved in for a kiss.

Jordan stilled for a moment but then seemed to melt under his touch, and he realized with a shock that Jordan was returning the kiss.

Oh my God.

Welcome to

Dreamspun Desires

Dear Reader,

Love is the dream. It dazzles us, makes us stronger, and brings us to our knees. Dreamspun Desires tell stories of love featuring your favorite heartwarming heroes, captivating plots, and exotic locations. Stories that make your breath catch and your imagination soar.

In the pages of these wonderful love stories, readers can escape to a world where love conquers all, the tenderness of a first kiss sweeps you away, and your heart pounds at the sight of the one you love.

When you put it all together, you find romance in its truest form.

Love always finds a way.

Elizabeth North

Executive Director
Dreamspinner Press

K.C. Wells

MY FAIR BRADY

PUBLISHED BY

DREAMSPINNER
PRESS

Published by
DREAMSPINNER PRESS

5032 Capital Circle SW, Suite 2, PMB# 279,
Tallahassee, FL 32305-7886 USA
www.dreamspinnerpress.com

This is a work of fiction. Names, characters, places, and incidents either
are the product of author imagination or are used fictitiously, and any
resemblance to actual persons, living or dead, business establishments,
events, or locales is entirely coincidental.

My Fair Brady
© 2019 K.C. Wells.
Editorial Development by Sue Brown-Moore.

Cover Art
© 2019 Alexandria Corza.
http://www.seeingstatic.com/
Cover content is for illustrative purposes only and any person depicted
on the cover is a model.

Paperback ISBN: 978-1-64108-142-9
Digital ISBN: 978-1-64405-005-7
Library of Congress Control Number: 2018960694
Paperback published February 2019
v. 1.0

Printed in the United States of America
∞
This paper meets the requirements of
ANSI/NISO Z39.48-1992 (Permanence of Paper).

K.C. WELLS started writing in 2012, although the idea of writing a novel had been in her head since she was a child. But after reading that first gay romance in 2009, she was hooked.

She now writes full-time, and the line of men in her head clamoring to tell their story is getting longer and longer. If the frequent visits by plot bunnies are anything to go by, that's not about to change anytime soon.

K.C. loves to hear from readers.
Email: k.c.wells@btinternet.com
Facebook: www.facebook.com/KCWellsWorld
Blog: kcwellsworld.blogspot.co.uk
Twitter: @K_C_Wells
Website: www.kcwellsworld.com
Instagram: www.instagram.com/k.c.wells

By K.C. Wells

DREAMSPUN DESIRES
#17 – The Senator's Secret
#40 – Out of the Shadows
#76 – My Fair Brady

Published by **DREAMSPINNER PRESS**
www.dreamspinnerpress.com

For Jason. This one needed a lot,
and you were AWESOME (as usual).

For my wonderful beta team.
Thank you SO MUCH
for your continuing support and advice.

Chapter One

"OKAY, you can put your shirt back on now." Dr. Peters put away his blood pressure monitor and sat behind his desk.

Jordan Wolf smiled as he did up his cuffs. "Any reason why you scheduled me for an appointment first thing on a Monday morning? Not that I'm complaining. At least this way, I get your perpetual nagging over sooner rather than later." He flashed the doctor a grin. Dr. Peters had been his physician for sixteen years, and they were pretty much used to each other.

Dr. Peters peered at him over his glasses. "So you already know what I'm about to say. Your blood pressure is still too high for my liking. And as for scheduling your appointment, it was deliberate. I like to ease into my workweek with patients who won't give me a headache. Mondays are enough of a ballache without that." He grinned. "By the way, I didn't schedule this appointment—your personal assistant did that. Because *you* don't schedule appointments."

Jordan put on his jacket and sat back in his chair. "I don't see what all the fuss is about. I don't think Mondays are so bad."

Dr. Peters gave a wry smile. "That's because your workweek isn't like most people's."

Jordan sighed. "And there you go, just like all the rest who think I have it easy. I don't sit back and let everyone else do the work, you know."

Dr. Peters arched his eyebrows. "Jordan, you're the CEO of one of the largest accounting firms in New York. I don't think for a second that you got to where you are without a lot of hard work, but I'm sure that by now you have things running just how you want them. The point is not about how stressful your work is—*my* point is about how many hours you spend in that office. How many business trips you take. How little time you spend in a gym. How much crap you're eating."

"I think my diet is just fine as it is. You should see the stuff I eat for lunch. All of it is healthy."

"I'm sure it is, only that's probably not down to you, is it? Someone orders in your food when you're in the office. At least that assistant has your best interests at heart," Dr. Peters remarked dryly. "It's what you eat *outside* of work that bothers me. And you know what I mean. You need to eat less salt. Less fat. Less red meat. More vegetables and greens." He sighed. "Look, the fact is, your blood pressure is too high. Period. So maybe you need to start thinking about making some changes."

Jordan sighed. "Such as what? I'm forty. It's not like I'm about to step down from the company."

"And I'm not suggesting that. But you need to do something. Otherwise, we are going to continue having this same conversation for a good while longer. And I don't want to get to the point where we're talking medication. Prevention is better than a cure, remember." Dr. Peters shook his head. "Why am I wasting my breath? You're already focused on tackling another week head-on. I know you too well."

Jordan rose to his feet. "I'll watch the diet, I'll try not to live in the office, and I'll attempt at least two sessions a week in the gym. Is that good enough for you?"

Dr. Peters laughed. "Jordan, this is me you're talking to. If you manage all that, I'll eat my prescription pad. Now, if you get your PA to schedule in a couple of gym visits and stick them on your calendar, *then* I'd believe you might actually get there. Now, get out of here and go run your company." He shook his head again. "Two sessions a week at the gym. Yeah, tell me another one."

He was still chuckling as Jordan left his office.

JORDAN smiled to himself as he stepped into the elevator. In spite of Dr. Peter's usual message of doom and gloom, he was feeling positive.

I have it pretty good. Not perfect, but yeah, pretty good.

Perfect would be having someone to share it all with, but he'd been there, tried that. Not one of his previous relationships had made it past two or three months. It had gotten to the point where Jordan was convinced every guy he met had read the same script:

"You work too hard." "You never have time for me." "I feel like I'm competing with your company."

Yeah, they just didn't get it. Success required effort. Time. Sweat. And all of that was nonnegotiable.

Jordan stepped out of the elevator and pushed open the glass door that led to his offices. Just like clockwork, there was Brady Donovan, his personal assistant, waiting for him, pushing his glasses higher onto the bridge of his nose as usual.

He handed Jordan a bundle of folded newspapers and magazines. "Good morning, sir. Here are your copies of the *Financial Times*, the *Wall Street Journal*, and the *Economist*. The *International Business Times* is already on your monitor, and I'll be in with your coffee in a moment."

"Thanks, Brady." Jordan went past him, along the hallway that was flanked by department offices, past the staff room, until he reached the door at the end. That was Brady's office. No one got to see Jordan without going through Brady, which was just how Jordan liked it. He walked past Brady's desk to the door of his office. Once inside, he strolled over to the wide desk, which was devoid of clutter, and sank into the high-backed leather chair behind it.

Seconds later, Brady was there with a coffee tray. He placed it on the desk and poured a cup. "When you're ready, sir, I'll go through your schedule for today and the rest of the week."

"Fine," Jordan said absently, already engrossed in the article on his monitor. By the time he'd read through the posts that interested him, forty minutes had passed, the coffeepot was empty, and he was ready for the day. The office door opened and Brady entered, tablet in hand.

Jordan smiled to himself. *He has my routine down to the second, doesn't he?* Sometimes he put Brady's uncanny sense of timing down to mind-reading.

"Your schedules are in your inbox, sir. You have a meeting at eleven with Paul Dudley, with regards to the new branch opening in Boston next month. There will be a conference call at two, with the manager of the Tallahassee branch. Those are the two most important points for today."

"Thanks, Brady." Jordan glanced at Brady's red bow tie. "Is that a new one?"

Brady smiled. "Not really. I've been wearing it for about two years now." He cleared his throat. "Will there be anything else?"

Jordan shook his head. "I'll call if I need anything. Besides, it looks like you have my day organized for me."

"Okay, sir."

It took Jordan a minute or two to realize Brady had left the room. Not that *that* was unusual—Brady seemed to come and go so quietly sometimes that Jordan was barely aware of his presence.

He was halfway through the *Financial Times* when his phone rang.

"Sir? Your mother is on line two."

"Thank you." Jordan pressed the button beside the blinking light. "Good morning, Mom."

"It is now," she commented, her voice decidedly cheerful. "The flowers just arrived. Jordan, they're beautiful. Thank you. And they smell divine."

For a second he was lost, but then he caught sight of his schedule: *Mom—birthday*. "I'm glad you like them. Sorry I didn't call you first thing. I was—"

"Sweetheart, I know how busy you are. Actually, I'm always surprised when you remember to send cards and gifts. You have so much to do, and yet you always manage to choose the perfect present. Your father still talks about that model ship kit you sent him for his birthday last year. Just what he wanted. And you know how much I love fragrant flowers. So difficult to find them—everything is reared in a hothouse for speed these days—but you do it every time." She paused. "Thank you again, darling. I'll let you get back to running your little empire." She laughed. "Nice to know that such a successful businessman still finds time to shop for his mother's birthday." She said her goodbyes and disconnected.

Jordan stared at the phone thoughtfully, then pressed the intercom. "Brady?"

"Sir?"

"What exactly did I send my mother for her birthday?"

"A hand-tied bouquet of roses, lilies, and freesia, sir. Oh, and a box of her favorite chocolate truffles."

Jordan blinked. "You know what my mom's favorite chocolates are?"

There was a small pause. "Of course. That's my job." Another pause. "Anything else, sir?"

"No, that will be all. Thank you, Brady." It wasn't until he'd finished the call that Jordan realized he should have thanked Brady for remembering her birthday. Because Jordan had completely forgotten.

Ten minutes later, his intercom buzzed. "Sir? Do you have time to go over the details for the Business & Financial Conference next week?"

It took Jordan a moment to recall the trip. Not that he was forgetful—conferences were solely Brady's terrain. "Sure, come on in."

A minute later, Brady was there, armed with his ever-present tablet.

Jordan gestured for him to sit on the couch. "Where *is* the conference again?" He had some vague recollection, but it had been months since he'd told Brady to book spots on it.

"At the Nashville Convention Center. We have rooms at the Renaissance Nashville Hotel. We fly in on Sunday morning, and the conference runs for three days. I've booked you in several of the breakout sessions, but I've made sure to schedule you some downtime too. There is also a preconference session on financial trends at one thirty on Sunday afternoon, and that's followed by the evening welcome reception."

"You've got the room next to mine as usual?"

Brady nodded. "And I'll be taking notes throughout the three days. I've also taken the liberty of booking you into the hotel spa." He smiled. "I know how much you like a good sauna and massage." He glanced at his tablet. "Our car to JFK is organized, as is the car when we land. I'll also liaise with Donna, to make sure she packs your tux—there are evening events planned for every night. There are networking continental breakfasts planned for each morning, but let me know if you want to skip them and I'll organize something to be brought to you."

"When do we fly home?" Jordan liked how he didn't have to concern himself with any of the details—Brady had taken care of everything, including getting his housekeeper, Donna, to do his packing.

"The conference concludes Wednesday before lunch. The flight will be roughly two and a half hours, so we should be back in New York in time for dinner."

"That all sounds great." Jordan smiled. "Just remind me ahead of—"

"I'll make sure you have all the details in writing, sir." Brady got up from the couch. "I'll be in my office if you need me." And with that, he left the room.

Jordan smiled to himself again. Brady had been with him for three years, and in all that time, his wardrobe hadn't varied in the slightest. His had a somewhat… muted style. He regularly wore beige chinos, with a white shirt and a pale cardigan, and always with a bow tie of some description. With clothing like that, Brady should have stood out, but remarkably, he seemed to fade into the background. That didn't make him any less efficient, however. Brady didn't fuss but merely got on with the job, and Jordan had to admit that things had gone smoothly around the office since his arrival.

He sincerely hoped Brady didn't decide to move on to greener pastures. Jordan doubted he could find another PA who was so damned easy to work with.

BRADY glanced at his phone. It was already seven o'clock, and Jordan was still there. *That man….* Brady sighed and shut down his computer, his gaze drifting to Jordan's door, through which came the tapping of keys. Brady got up and went over to it, then paused as he listened. *Come on, Jordan. Time to call it a day.*

He knocked quietly and waited. When there was no response, he ducked his head around the door. Jordan was at his desk, typing on his keyboard, his brow furrowed. He wore his earbuds, which accounted for the lack of response. Brady walked over to the desk and stood in front of it.

Jordan glanced up and gave a start. "Christ!" He pulled the earbuds from his ears and gave Brady a hard stare. "Do you have to sneak up on me like that? Did you want something?"

Brady sighed. "One, it was hardly sneaking, and two, have you glanced out of the window lately?" When Jordan's frown deepened, Brady shook his head. "Everyone went home an hour ago."

Jordan peered at his monitor. "Is that the time?" He sagged in his chair. "I started making notes for an article in the *Economist*, and I guess I got carried away."

"I'll call your car service, sir. They'll be here in about ten minutes." Thankfully they were used to Jordan's timekeeping by now.

"Thank you."

"Donna will have left for the day, so I'll arrange for dinner to be delivered. It should be there not long after you get home." *Home* was a two-bedroom apartment on East Eighty-Second Street in the Upper East Side of Manhattan, nearly thirty streets—and a whole world— away from Brady's place. Jordan didn't really need a housekeeper with a property that size, but once Brady had started working for him, it hadn't taken him all that long to realize his boss needed looking after.

He probably has no idea what I do on a daily basis to make sure his company—and his life—runs smoothly.

Brady walked behind the desk, peered at the screen, and saved Jordan's notes. Then he shut down the computer. "Come on, sir. Time to go home," he said gently.

Jordan smiled. "What would I do without you, Brady?"

As much as Brady did for him, he knew there was no such thing as an indispensable man. If he walked out the following day, Jordan could easily find someone to replace him. Not that he had any such plans. Brady loved his job. He loved putting his organizational skills to good use.

Then there was the tiny but not insignificant fact that he was crushing on his boss.

And he will never, ever find that out. Because that would be a disaster in the making.

Chapter Two

"HEY, Jordan! I thought I'd missed you."

Jordan smiled at the familiar voice, then turned to greet Drake Daniels. "And I thought it weird not to have seen you before today." He shook his head. "Cutting it fine, Drake." The conference would finish later that day, and Jordan had come to the networking breakfast to catch up with a few of his business acquaintances. Drake Daniels, however, was more of a friend. They'd gone to college together, and although their paths diverged, they'd kept in touch.

Drake laughed. "I usually skip these breakfasts. It's too damn early for power talks." He patted Jordan on the arm. "So, how is life in the Big Apple? Still aiming to be on the Fortune 500?"

Jordan chuckled. "No such aspirations, but I'm doing well. I take it you're doing well?"

"The business is ticking over. I can't complain," Drake said with a modest shrug. Jordan knew better. Drake was doing very well indeed.

"How are Belinda and the kids?"

Drake's face glowed. "Great. Marty and Dawn are in high school now, and Belinda's gotten involved in a lot of charity work." His eyes widened. "Actually, I was going to call you. It's our fifteenth wedding anniversary next month, and we're having a weekend party at our place in the Hamptons. I was going to invite you to join us."

"Aw, that's great. I'd have to look at my calendar, of course."

"Sure. I'll send an invite for you and a plus-one." Drake's eyes gleamed. "Anyone special on the horizon I should know about?"

Jordan shook his head. "Sorry. Nothing to tell."

Drake stroked his chin. "Hmm. There's a guy in my PR department that would be right up your alley. Are you into blonds?"

"To be honest I don't really go for a particular type. And no, you are *not* going to set me up with anyone. Rest assured, I'll be bringing a guest." Jordan made a mental note to call Clive. His first college roommate was always up for a party, and they got along really well. And if it kept Drake from arranging a hookup…. He knew Drake's ways of old. There was always the chance that he'd remember Clive from back then, but it was a risk Jordan was willing to take.

"Excellent. I look forward to seeing you there." Drake peered over his shoulder. "Don't look now, but there's a geeky guy hovering behind you, like he's waiting to claim your attention."

Jordan glanced around and smiled. "Be nice. That 'geeky guy,' as you put it, is the best damn personal assistant I've ever had."

Drake bit his lip. "My apologies. What he lacks in appearance, he obviously makes up for in efficiency."

Jordan couldn't help feeling somewhat irked. "Ever heard the saying 'Don't judge a book by its cover'? So what *you're* saying is, I should have some dishy guy working for me, who probably can't do a quarter of what Brady does but who provides me with eye candy around the office? Give me someone like Brady every time. He's reliable, trustworthy—and yes, he's goddamn efficient."

Drake held up his hands as if to placate him. "Again, my apologies. I seem to have hit a nerve. I hope you'll still accept the invitation to the party. It'll be a lot of fun, and I know Belinda would love to see you again."

Slightly mollified, Jordan sighed. "We'll see. And now I'd better find out what Brady wants. Good to see you again, Drake." They shook hands, and Jordan turned to face Brady.

"I didn't mean to interrupt, sir, but you've had an email that requires your immediate attention," Brady said apologetically.

Jordan waved a hand. "You weren't interrupting." He took the tablet Brady proffered and scanned the email. "Thanks. You were right. Email them back and tell them they can go ahead." He gestured to a table. "Have you had breakfast?"

Brady smiled. "I grabbed a cup of coffee in my room." He grimaced. "The less said about that, the better."

Jordan pulled out a chair. "Then sit. I'll fetch you a decent cup of coffee and some pastries." Brady started to protest, but Jordan shook his head. "Pardon my bluntness, but you've worked your ass off these last three days. And seeing as I'm being honest…." He peered closely at Brady, noting his pallor and the lines around his eyes. "Are you feeling okay?"

Brady's smile faded. "Not exactly. I… I didn't sleep well, and I'm not feeling 100 percent."

That did it. Jordan indicated the chair. "Sit. You're going to have some breakfast, and then you're going to take the rest of the morning off until we leave." He cocked his head to one side. "You've already packed my bag, haven't you?"

"Well, checkout *is* at eleven. I've left out your toiletries in your bathroom, but yes, you're all set." Brady sat down.

"Perfect. Then you sit tight while I get you that coffee I promised." Jordan grinned. "Which is probably way better than what passes for coffee in our rooms." He left Brady and went over to the buffet. As he filled a cup, Jordan realized Drake's comments still bothered him.

What does it matter what Brady looks like? He gets the job done.

Jordan always liked to dress sharply, but that didn't mean he was a slave to the latest fashion. He liked good-quality, well-fitted suits and no-nonsense ties in a solid color. So what if Brady had a style that was all his own? It worked fine for the office, so what was the problem?

Jordan glanced over to where Brady sat, studying his tablet. Today's bow tie was a deep bronze that seemed to go with his eyes. Then Jordan shook himself.

Since when do I notice his eyes?

THE driver took Jordan's luggage and suit bags, then placed them in the trunk. Jordan gestured toward the rear of the car. "Yours too."

Brady shook his head. "I'll get the train."

Jordan gave him a mock glare. "You most certainly will not. Uh-uh. Not when I have a car ready to take me home. We can drop you off too."

"You're not going my way," Brady protested. He didn't need this, not when he was still feeling like shit.

"Where do you live?"

"Nowhere near the Upper East Side," Brady fired back. He sighed. "I'm sorry. That was rude."

Jordan regarded him closely. "You still don't feel so good, do you? Well, we're dropping you off, so deal with it." He nodded to the driver. "His bag too, please."

Brady was in no shape to argue. Besides, he knew better. Jordan wasn't about to take no for an answer. Then a horrible thought occurred to him. "What if I'm coming down with something and I infect you?"

Jordan opened the rear door. "Get in." He smiled. "And I'll open a window."

There was nothing to do but comply.

Brady got into the car and sank thankfully against the leather seat. Maybe this was better than taking the train after all. Jordan got in beside him and gazed at him expectantly. It took Brady's befuddled brain a moment to realize he was waiting for the address. "West 111th Street, near Lenox Avenue. Harlem."

Jordan blinked but then nodded before passing it along to the driver. The car pulled away from the curb, and they left the airport behind them.

"How long have you lived in Harlem?" Jordan asked after they'd been traveling for a while. Traffic on the 678 wasn't that bad as they headed through Queens.

"Since I started working for you," Brady replied. "Before that I had this teeny little apartment in the East Village. Not that this place is all that much bigger, but it's right around the corner from Central Park, and it's handy for the subway."

"Is it just you, or do you share?"

Brady chuckled. "Just me. There's one bedroom. And I've had my share of weird roommates, so no, not gonna do *that* again. It might cost me more, but it's worth it for the peace and quiet." Not that he'd brought anyone back there. *And how sad is that?* Brady rested his aching head against the seat and closed his eyes, hoping Jordan would forgive him. He wasn't being rude. He just didn't have the energy or the willpower to indulge in small talk.

What the hell is wrong with me? He'd been right as rain the previous day, but this had come down on him like a ton of bricks with no warning. Brady fervently hoped an early night with some Tylenol and whatever else he could find in his medicine cabinet would do the trick, because *no way* was he about to miss a day of work.

Brady might not be indispensable, but when it came to knowing Jordan's ways inside and out, he doubted there was anyone else in that building who could keep his boss on track.

THURSDAY already? After three days of conferences, Jordan was more than ready to get back to work. He exited the elevator, pushed open the door, and—

No Brady.

Jordan stopped dead in his tracks.

Celia, the receptionist at the front desk, gave him a knowing glance. "Yeah, he called in sick about a half hour ago. I don't think I've ever known Brady to take a sick day."

Jordan had never known it either, not that he was totally surprised. He'd figured whatever Brady had come down with in Nashville, it had to be pretty virulent, judging by the speed with which Brady had succumbed. By the time they'd dropped Brady outside his building the previous evening, he'd been almost wilting. He was still stubborn enough to refuse Jordan's offer of help up to his apartment, however.

"Can I get you anything, Mr. Wolf?" Celia asked with a bright smile. "Coffee, perhaps?"

"Thank you, that would be great." Jordan walked along the hallway, noting the conversations already taking place in several of the offices. He entered Brady's office and stilled at the sight of the empty desk. Not having Brady there felt… weird. Jordan went through to his own office, dropped his briefcase on the couch, and strolled over to the large expanse of glass that offered a view of the Manhattan skyline. North of there was Brady, in God knew what state.

Get well soon, Jordan said silently, aiming his thoughts in the general direction of Harlem.

"Your coffee, sir." Celia placed a tray on his desk and withdrew.

Jordan poured himself a cup, then switched on his laptop. It was only then that he realized he was missing something: there were no newspapers on his desk.

Jordan shook his head. *It's not as if I can't find a copy of the* FT *somewhere.*

It took him a moment to realize that he had no idea if Brady had them delivered or if he picked them up on his way to work or what. Having them waiting for him on arrival had become as second nature as... getting dressed in the morning.

Jordan took a sip of coffee and grimaced. It was slightly bitter and nothing like his regular coffee. He buzzed Celia's intercom. "Celia? As a matter of interest, what coffee am I drinking?"

There was a moment of silence. "Er, the same coffee we all drink, sir?" she said slowly. "It came from the coffeepot in the staff room."

One thing was clear: wherever Brady got his coffee, it certainly wasn't there. "Okay, thanks, Celia." He took one look at the dark brown liquid and shuddered. *Have I become a coffee snob? Is that it?* Then he shook his head. Brady had obviously found a coffee that Jordan liked and stuck to that, though where he kept it was anybody's guess.

Jordan opened his weekly schedule, thankful to have some idea of what the day held in store for him. It wasn't the same as the detailed daily notes Brady usually provided, but it would do at a pinch.

God, I hope he's back to work tomorrow.

The thought made him chuckle aloud. Had he become so reliant on Brady that he couldn't cope on his own? It was just a change in coffee, an absence of newspapers, and a not-so-detailed schedule, for God's sake.

Time to just deal with it.

Jordan had a company to run, and he'd managed just fine before Brady had even put his nose through the door. He had no doubt that he would manage just fine now.

Chapter Three

JORDAN glanced at his phone for the tenth time in about the last half hour. *Where the hell is my lunch?* No delivery, no box of something that managed to be nutritious *and* delicious—which was a minor miracle in Jordan's book, because in his experience, healthy food bore more than a passing resemblance to cardboard. Yet what arrived in his office every day like clockwork was amazing.

Only today? It hadn't. Obviously someone's clock was busted.

When it got to an hour later and still no lunch, Jordan got up and walked into Brady's office, staring at his desk as if that would tell him something. He couldn't for the life of him figure out what the problem was. There'd been a delivery on Thursday and Friday, and Brady had been off sick then. So what the hell was wrong with Monday's delivery?

Then it came to him. The previous week's lunches had been organized by Brady *before* he came down with the flu. And then the full force of that revelation hit: there would be no lunches delivered as long as Brady was off sick.

Well, shit.

Jordan hadn't been having the best of days up until that point. This new knowledge just took a dump on the rest of his week. His stomach growled, and that was just a reminder of what hadn't arrived. Jordan retreated into his office, buzzed Celia, and asked her to organize some sandwiches or something. *Anything*.

When his intercom flashed, it was Celia, not with news of the impending arrival of food, but to announce a call from his sister. *Great. That's all I need.* With a sigh, Jordan connected the call.

"Hey, what's up?"

Fiona chuckled. "Good to hear you too. You sound miserable. You okay?"

He stifled another sigh. "Fi, to what do I owe the pleasure? Not that I'm unhappy to get a call from my little sister, but now is not a good time."

Her voice softened. "Aw, what's wrong? I only called to say I went to see Mom on her birthday, and I saw the flowers you sent her. They're gorgeous. You can smell them as soon as you go into the house." Another wry chuckle. "Definitely scored yourself a point with those."

"Except I didn't send them. Or the chocolates. That would be Brady, my personal assistant."

"Wow. Obviously a man with taste. Pass him my compliments."

Jordan huffed. "I would, but he's off sick."

There was a pause. "Okay, Jordan, out with it. What's going on?"

He leaned back in his chair, the phone cradled against his ear. "I guess I'm having a bad day, that's all." More like a bad *three* days, and it certainly didn't look like there'd be an improvement anytime soon.

"Why? What's happened?"

Jordan snickered. "It's more a case of what *hasn't* happened. That man goes off sick for *three days*, and the place is falling down around my ears. Okay, maybe that's an exaggeration, but that's how it feels."

"For example?"

He sighed inwardly. *Where do I start?* "My lunch didn't arrive today."

Fiona snorted. "Why—did it miss the bus or something?"

"Do you know how long it took me to work out that Brady hadn't ordered it? He organizes all my meals that come into the office. He even makes sure they're healthy. I swear, he and Dr. Peters are in cahoots with each other."

"Good for him. *Someone* has to watch out for you. Is that it? Your company's falling down around your ears because you got no lunch?" She snickered.

"I wish. No, what's really hit home during the three days he's been off so far is just how much he does around here—for me. It might be my company, but it's Brady Donovan who keeps my routine moving like clockwork." That realization had certainly given Jordan's self-confidence a knock.

"How?"

"I *know* he organizes the cars that take me everywhere. I *know* he sets up my meetings and works out my schedule. It's all the rest, the stuff that goes on that I never get to see. Take this morning as a for instance. I spent the whole morning going through all the reports from the department heads. You wouldn't believe how much crap I had to wade through in order to get to the important stuff."

"Well, don't you usually do that?"

"No! That's my point. *Brady* reads through all that, then decides what I need to see. Not only that, he sends out memos to those departments without troubling me about them. And when I arrived here this morning, the first person in my office was a department chief, asking when the new assistants were starting work. *I* didn't know we were taking on new assistants. That was when I learned that Brady usually deals with the lower-level hiring, because apparently it's a need-to-know situation, and *I* don't need to know about it. And to be honest? After the headache I got trying to sort out the issue, I'm grateful for Brady taking those matters out of my hands."

"He sounds very efficient."

"That's just it. He does his job, quickly and efficiently. Take Mom's flowers. Okay, I'll admit, I'd totally forgotten it was her birthday until she called to thank me for the flowers. But it wasn't just her. He sends gifts to clients without me ever having to think about it. He sorts out all the press interviews and articles." Jordan sighed again. "And the latest fiasco was just another example of how much he does."

"Fiasco? That doesn't sound good."

"The biannual raises and promotions weren't published. See, what usually happens is Brady reviews everything, like I told him to, then brings the lists to me for approval. I just okay it without question because he's already gone through it all and I know it will be fair and accurate. Only—"

"Only, he's not there to publish the lists, is he? So it didn't get done." Fiona sighed too. "Yeah, don't lose this guy. He sounds amazing."

"He's doing exactly what I asked him to when I hired him. I told him I wanted things to run like clockwork, and I didn't want my day cluttered with minutiae." Brady had taken him at his word, it seemed. After one day of trying to sort out who was due for a raise/promotion, Jordan's blood pressure had climbed, and he'd taken a couple of Tylenol to deal with his thumping headache.

If this is what life is like after three days, imagine what state my health would be in if Brady hadn't been there. Jordan guessed Dr. Peters would really have grounds to worry.

There was a knock at the door, and Celia stuck her head around it. Jordan wanted to sigh with relief when he saw the box in her hands, but he'd done way too much sighing in Fiona's ear already.

"Hey, sis, my lunch has arrived."

"Thank God for that. Go eat. Maybe you'll be less growly after."

"Growly?"

She laughed. "You wanna know what I think? The best thing that could happen to you is for this Brady to come back to work. Because it sounds to me like you really need him."

Jordan couldn't agree more.

After lunch, he had a quick meeting with the four department heads, just to make sure everything was on track. Thankfully, for the first time that day, things appeared to be running more smoothly.

Dan Fremont lingered after the other heads had left the office. "Are you doing okay, Mr. Wolf?"

Jordan snickered. "Why do you ask? Do I look as frazzled as I feel?"

Dan laughed. "Let me guess. You're missing Brady."

"Does it show that much?" Jordan sagged into his chair. "Talk about not knowing how much you've got till it's gone."

"Yeah, I can understand that. Brady's extremely… capable."

"That's one word for him."

Dan chuckled. "You better keep hold of that guy. And I know you might not wanna think about it, but if you ever decide you could survive without him as your PA, he'd make a fantastic exec. He might only have been here three years, but he knows how this company runs— and what it takes to keep it running efficiently." Dan smiled. "Best decision you ever made, taking him on."

Jordan arched his eyebrows. "So glad you approve," he remarked dryly.

Dan flushed. "I didn't mean it to come out like that. But it's not just me who thinks that way. We all deal with Brady every day, and we've been here long enough to remember what life was like before he arrived. You work damn hard, Mr. Wolf. Having someone alongside you to share the workload? That's gotta be a good thing." He gave Jordan a single nod, then left the office.

Jordan got up from his desk and walked over to the door that led to Brady's office. He stared at the empty chair. It was gratifying to know his staff thought so highly of Brady. And Dan was right. Jordan intended keeping hold of Brady for as long as he could. And if that meant promoting him? At least he knew there'd be no objections.

I hope he's back tomorrow.

WHEN Wednesday evening arrived, along with an email to say Brady wouldn't be back at work for the remainder of the week, Jordan decided to take matters into his own hands. When his car arrived, Jordan told him to take a detour via Harlem.

He wasn't really sure why he was going there. Did he *really* need Brady to sort out the increasing number of problems arriving on his desk? Or was it more a case that, deep down, Jordan was concerned about his PA? And what did he expect Brady to do when he got there—shrug off whatever was ailing him and sort out Jordan's problems?

This last thought made him pause as he sent away the car, having no real idea how long he'd be there. He could always get a taxi home. Jordan sighed. When had he last taken a taxi? And what he was about to do started to sound like a really bad, selfish move on his part. The man was *ill*, for God's sake.

Jordan stared at the light brown wood door with its inset glass panels. *Well, I'm here now. Might as well find out what's wrong with him.* He was about to ring the bell, when the door opened and a young woman came out.

"Excuse me, I'm looking for apartment 2B. Brady Donovan."

She nodded. "Second floor. Is he okay? I haven't seen much of him lately." She narrowed her gaze. "Who are you?"

"His boss. And he's ill. I've just come over to check up on him." He could understand her apprehension. After all, he was a stranger to her. Her suspicious gaze hadn't altered, so he took out his wallet. "Did you know Brady works for Jordan Wolf Accounting?" When she nodded, he withdrew his ID and held it up for inspection.

The young woman's eyes widened. "Oh. You really *are* his boss. Okay. I'll let you in. Just be sure you don't give him any grief. He's sweet. Tell him hey from Phil on the third floor." When Jordan stared at her, she rolled her eyes. "Well, I'm hardly gonna stick with Philomena, am I? Parents and their ideas…." She held open the front door for him. "Go straight up the stairs. He's on the left."

"Thanks—*Phil*," Jordan said with a smile.

She laughed. "Just be sure to say hi for me." She glanced at his hands, empty but for his briefcase. "Where's the chicken noodle soup? That's what you bring if someone's ill, my mom always says."

Jordan gave a guilty start. She had a point.

Let's see what he needs first.

He thanked her again and proceeded up the wide staircase to the second floor. There were two apartments, and Brady's door was painted a glossy black, with a spy hole set into it. Jordan rapped on the door, listening for any movement within.

Nothing.

He rapped again. This time he caught a shuffling sound, growing louder, then a bolt being drawn back, the click of a lock….

The door swung open, and Brady stood there, wrapped in a comforter, holding on to the doorframe. "What are you doing here?" he croaked. His hair was unkempt and his forehead glistened. Dark circles shadowed his eyes, and he looked like he was about to fall over at any moment.

Jordan didn't waste a second. "Looking after you, it seems." He stepped into the apartment, a long room with beautiful hardwood floors and one wall of red brick. From the look of things, Brady had been lying on the couch, which was covered in blankets and pillows. DVD cases were scattered over the floor, but the TV was off.

Jordan put his arm around Brady's shoulders and guided him back to the couch. "Now lie down before you *fall* down," he said firmly. Brady dropped onto the cushions like a stone, and Jordan grabbed the blankets to cover him. "Have you seen a doctor?"

Brady gave a single nod. "Flu. Apparently there's a... nasty strain going around New York." He broke off to cough, his face reddening.

Jordan had seen the reports on the news. "Brady, people are dying from that one!"

"Yeah, well, I'm not." Brady gave another racking cough. "I thought a few days... in bed would do the trick... but I guess not."

Jordan perched on the edge of the seat cushion, shaking his head. "Real flu—not some bad cold—puts you on your ass for at least a couple of weeks." He reached to push Brady's hair back from his forehead, but Brady tried to shrink away.

"No... you shouldn't be here.... You'll catch it...." Another fit of coughing erupted, followed by a violent bout of sneezing, and Brady grabbed the box of tissues from their spot on the floor beside the couch.

Jordan regarded him closely. "No, I won't. Well, I *probably* won't. My doctor made me get the flu shot a couple of weeks ago, so I'm less likely to catch it." He glanced around the room. There was a tiny kitchen area with a stove, fitted into a corner. The lack of dishes—

dirty or otherwise—led to a growing suspicion. "Have you been eating properly? Is there anyone who can come over here to make sure you're all right?"

Brady huffed. "Like I'm gonna... call on my neighbors... just so I can give them the flu."

Jordan folded his arms. "What have you been eating?"

Brady shrugged. "Ramen, mostly. Toast. Tea. That's about it."

Jordan had heard enough. He got to his feet. "Okay, I need to go buy a few things, but I'll be back." Brady struggled to sit up, his expression alarmed, but Jordan gently but firmly pressed him back down. "And *you* are going to lie there and do nothing until I return. Except maybe drink a lot of fluids." He walked over to the cabinet above the sink, found a clean glass, and filled it with water. Then he took it over to the couch and placed it on the floor within reach. "I want to see that all gone by the time I get back."

Brady narrowed his gaze. "Excuse me? Did you perhaps mistake my apartment for your office?" Whatever else he was going to say was lost in a coughing fit.

"See? That's what you get for trying to sass the boss. Now do as you're told, mister."

Brady gazed up at him, his forehead still slick with sweat. "Yes, sir."

Jordan found the bathroom, wrung out a cloth under the faucet, then returned to Brady's side. He crouched down next to the couch and gently wiped Brady's brow. "That's better, isn't it?" Jordan said softly.

Brady swallowed. "Yes, sir," he whispered.

Jordan placed the cloth in his hand and rose to walk over to the door.

"Sir?"

Jordan stopped and turned. "Brady. We're not in the office, as you so succinctly pointed out. So call me Jordan, okay?"

Brady nodded. "Hook by the door. My keys. The one with the yellow tab. And the code for the main door key pad is one-two-five-seven." He paused, swallowing once more. "And... thank you... Jordan."

"You're welcome." Jordan grabbed the keys and left the apartment. As he walked down the stairs, he got out his phone and pulled up a search engine.

Knowing what stores were available in Brady's neighborhood was probably a good place to start.

BRADY waited until he was sure Jordan had gone before throwing back the comforter, hoisting himself off the couch, and stumbling over to the bathroom. No way was he about to pee while Jordan was there—the door didn't shut properly.

When he'd finished, he leaned on the sink and stared at his reflection in the mirror. Christ, he looked a mess. He wondered briefly if he had time to take a shower before Jordan got back, but reasoned he didn't have the energy to stand for that long. Brady sniffed cautiously and grimaced. He smelled disgusting. Okay, maybe not a shower, but at least he could sit on the toilet and manage a quick washup. Anything to get rid of the smell of stale sweat.

Once he'd done the best he could, Brady shuffled into the bedroom in search of a clean pair of sweats and a T-shirt. His body ached like a son of a bitch, and somewhere in his head, a tiny band was stomping and beating out a military tattoo. The flu had well and truly kicked his butt.

He sank back onto the couch, pulling the comforter over him as he shivered. Thank God the couch was near the radiator. He popped the cap on the bottle of Tylenol and chugged a couple down with water. Then he closed his eyes, lamenting that of all the people to see him in such a sad state, why did it *have* to be the one man who frequented Brady's dreams?

God sure had a weird sense of humor.

Chapter Four

JORDAN carried the two bulging plastic bags up the steps to the front door, then put one of them down on the doorstep while he keyed in the code. Why the hell couldn't Brady live somewhere with more stores? He'd finally found what he wanted—three blocks over and eleven streets down, on Columbus Avenue—but that had necessitated a taxi. Both ways. And thank God the store was still open; it was getting late.

Jordan arrived at Brady's door, fumbled in his pants for the keys, and finally got into the apartment. Brady was asleep on the couch, his glasses still perched on his nose. All the lights were off, except for a lamp beside him. As quietly as he could, Jordan crept over to the tall refrigerator and began to fill it with his purchases. He'd bought enough to see Brady through at least the next three days or so, not that Jordan planned on staying away *that* long.

"Wha…?"

Jordan turned around. Brady had propped himself up on one elbow and was blinking at him. "Sorry," Jordan apologized. "It took me a little longer than I'd anticipated."

Brady stared at the bags. "You went to… the Whole Foods Market? Which one?"

"I figured the one on Columbus was closer than the one on 125th Street." Jordan turned back to the fridge and continued unpacking his groceries. He snickered. "Probably not that much to choose between them, when you think about it."

"You didn't walk all that way, did you?" Brady's voice was laced with incredulity.

Jordan chuckled. "I took a cab." When silence fell, he peered over his shoulder to find Brady gaping at him. "What? I've taken cabs before."

Brady chuckled. "Not since I joined the company. I'm the one who books your car service, remember?"

Jordan ignored that last remark. "Okay, when I'm done unpacking, I've got some soup for you, which you're going to eat before you go to bed. There's a good selection of fruit here, too, and vegetables. I picked out a couple of cartons of freshly made pasta and sauce to go with it. Oh, and there's juice too." He'd tried to choose food that wouldn't require much preparation.

"Wow. You really went to a lot of trouble for me," Brady said quietly. "I don't know what to say." Then he frowned. "Wait a minute. Have *you* eaten yet?"

Jordan shrugged. "I grabbed a burger and some fries. I'll heat 'em up when I get home."

Brady's eyes widened. "You're not supposed to eat shit like that." When Jordan stared at him, Brady flushed. "Why do you think your food at work is always so healthy? I'm trying to watch your diet, to keep your blood pressure in check."

"Well, just once won't kill me, so deal with it." Jordan went back to filling the refrigerator. "And seeing as you're so concerned, why don't I ditch the burger and share some soup with you instead?"

Brady blinked again. "Oh... okay. I can live with that."

Jordan shook his head. "Trying to organize my life from your sickbed, huh?" He snickered. "Well, guess what? When I finish work tomorrow, I'm coming here again. I'm going to make sure you eat properly at least once a day."

Brady let out a throaty chuckle. "You just want me back at work ASAP, don't you?"

Jordan rolled his eyes. "Of course! How the hell do you expect me to get through my week without you there, sorting out the mess?" He grinned.

Brady laughed softly. "I was afraid to ask how things were going. How did the meeting go yesterday with Roy McCullock?"

Jordan closed the door of the refrigerator. "You mean, the meeting that wasn't on my schedule? The meeting I didn't know about until his secretary called me?"

Brady gaped. "But... I told you weeks ago about that. It was in your planner. Did you even look there?"

"Well... no."

"And I reminded you about it at least a half-dozen times. Plus, there's a Post-it on your blotter."

Jordan sighed inwardly. He hadn't even looked. He was so used to Brady telling him every morning, he hadn't bothered to do more than a cursory glance when he got into the office, too desperate for a decent cup of coffee to even get his brain engaged.

He came over to the couch and sat down. "I'm sorry. You're right, of course. I should have looked. It's my business, my responsibility. I've just gotten so used to the way you do things, I guess." He smiled. "It's taken this past week to show me what you really are."

"And what's that?" Brady asked, his voice hushed.

"A treasure. And that's why I'll be here after work tomorrow, and the next day, and on the weekend, to do all I can to help you mend." Jordan peered at the glass beside the couch. "I thought I told you to drink all that water."

Brady bit his lip. "That's my second glass." Then he sagged against the cushions.

Jordan picked up the cloth, poured a little water onto it, then placed it on Brady's forehead. "You look after me in so many ways, so I guess it's only right that I look after you."

When Brady's eyes glistened, Jordan's throat tightened.

"Thank you… Jordan. Seriously." Brady cleared his throat. "Can I ask… what kind of soup are we having?"

Jordan smiled. "As recommended by Phil on the third floor, chicken noodle." Then an awful thought occurred to him. "Oh, Lord—please tell me you're not a vegetarian or vegan or something like that."

Brady shook his head. "All those times we went on business trips, and you never *once* paid attention to what I was eating?" He flashed a grin. "Relax. I'm a regular little omnivore."

Jordan wiped his brow dramatically. "Thank heavens." He tilted his head to one side. "But you're right. I should have noticed. I promise to do better from now on." He lurched across the floor and grabbed the box of little pouches from the countertop, holding it up for Brady to see. "Theraflu. I'll mix one up for you. This should help you feel a lot better. You can take this now, and then I'll heat up the soup. And the bakery had the most amazing-smelling rolls. I got some of those too. I got butter as well, just in case you didn't have any."

Brady smiled. "I feel better already." He coughed, his face red again.

"Yes, I can see that," Jordan commented dryly. "No more talking for a while. Let's get you fed." He began the task of preparing the Theraflu.

Brady needed taking care of, and Jordan aimed to make sure that happened.

BRADY opened his eyes and peered at the clock beside his bed. He'd fallen asleep the instant his head had hit the pillow. He guessed from the hour and the silence in the apartment that Jordan had left.

Brady still couldn't believe Jordan had turned up like that. At first he was convinced Jordan had come by merely to check that he really was sick. Then he thought maybe Jordan had visited to pick Brady's brains about work. Neither turned out to be true. Jordan hadn't spoken about work, other than the reference to the meeting that almost never was. Instead, he made sure Brady ate all his soup, and then he'd gone into the bedroom, found fresh linens, and changed the sheets. Brady had gotten into bed that night surrounded by the clean smell of cotton.

A shower would have to wait until he could stand in it without his legs shaking like they were made of Jell-O.

What do you know? Jordan Wolf turns out to be a really nice guy. Not that Brady had thought otherwise, but it was good to know the inside matched the exterior. His brain dimly recalled Jordan saying something about coming back the next few evenings, but Brady wasn't going to hold his breath. Jordan had enough to do running his company without spending time with a sick employee.

Still, it was a pleasant thought. Jordan had a nice bedside manner, and the way he'd stocked Brady's refrigerator and cabinets? Just… wow. Brady had no idea how he could ever repay him.

The last thing to flit through his fevered mind before he fell asleep was that he wished he hadn't been so ill. That way, he might actually have remembered more of Jordan's visit. Because having him that close had been wonderful.

BRADY tottered out of the bathroom, wrapped in his bathrobe. He was still pretty wobbly on his feet, although his aches had dissipated a little since he'd been taking the Theraflu. Twenty-four hours since Jordan had dropped by, and Brady was starting to feel a bit more human.

The door buzzed, and he shuffled over to the intercom. "Hello?"

"Brady, it's Jordan."

Brady stared at the gray plastic intercom box. *Really?* So it hadn't been just talk after all.

The door buzzed again, and Brady realized Jordan was still waiting down on the street. "Letting you in." He held down the door release button, waiting until he'd given Jordan enough time to get inside, then glanced down at his attire. Shit. There wasn't enough time to get some clothes on before Jordan would be—

There was a rap on his door.

Chuckling, Brady opened it. "You could have used the code, you know."

"I didn't want to surprise you."

It was then that Brady was hit by a delicious aroma. "Oh my God, that smells awesome."

Jordan held up a bag. "I hope you don't mind. I thought I'd eat here with you."

Brady stared. "Red Rooster? What made you go there? Not that I'm complaining—I *love* eating there."

"I asked the chauffeur if he could recommend any decent places for takeout around here. It turns out he was brought up in Harlem. Red Rooster was the first place he suggested."

Brady couldn't stop smiling. "Do I smell... fried chicken?" His stomach grumbled, and Brady's face heated up. "Sorry about that. Guess it's been a while since I ate."

That earned him a hard stare. "What did I say about taking care of yourself?"

"Aw, please. Don't give me a hard time." Brady gave him a hopefully appealing glance. "I'm sick, remember?"

Jordan laughed. "Not too sick to try puppy-dog eyes, I see. Well, I suppose sick PAs get to have fried chicken, mac and greens, and honey biscuits."

It took every ounce of Brady's willpower not to drool.

Jordan gazed at his robe, and Brady coughed. "Let me put something on while you put out the food, okay? I just took a shower."

Jordan narrowed his gaze. "Was that wise?"

Brady rolled his eyes. "Trust me, I smelled so bad, even the cockroaches fled." He walked carefully across the floor to his bedroom. "I can feel you watching me, you know," he called out without turning. "I *can* get around my own apartment."

"Glad to hear it. That means you're feeling better, right?"

Brady couldn't miss the hopeful note in Jordan's voice. He paused at his bedroom door. "I'll be back at work before you know it, and then you'll be wondering why you ever tried to hurry me back there, when I'm complaining about the mess you let things get into while I was gone."

As he closed the door, he caught Jordan's muttered, "Who says they're a mess?"

Brady laughed silently. He knew better.

By the time he left his bedroom, Jordan had plated up the meal, and the aroma filled the small apartment. Jordan was shaking his head. "I thought mac and greens sounded healthy."

Brady snickered. "It has braised collards and bok choy. They're green."

"Yeah, right, and the rest. There's cheddar in here, gruyère, parmesan, and… is that bacon and cream too?" Jordan gave him another hard stare. "And you were giving *me* a hard time over my diet?"

Brady laughed. "I said I love the food. I don't eat there all that often, however." He gave Jordan a warm smile. "This is… wonderful. Thank you." And this was the best he'd felt all day.

Jordan waited until he was seated on the couch before passing him his plate. "You look brighter. Better than last night, at any rate."

"I was a good boy today. I drank plenty of juice, I took my Theraflu religiously, and I ate a couple of pieces of fruit, plus some of the pasta." Brady sighed. "But I have to be honest. I still feel really weak."

"You will," Jordan said, nodding. "Like I said, the flu knocks you on your ass. And I'm *not* trying to hurry you back into work. Jordan Wolf Accounting had been in business for ten years before you came to work for me. I'm pretty sure it can survive another week or so of your absence." His dark eyes gleamed with amusement.

Brady didn't answer. He was too busy taking a mouthful of delicious fried chicken. Then Jordan's words registered. "Another week or so?"

Jordan nodded again. "You take as long as you need to, okay?" Then he smiled, and it lit up his handsome face. "Just as long as you know… I'm going to be *so* happy when you walk into the office."

He wouldn't be the only one. Brady loved his job, and that was mostly due to his gorgeous boss. It didn't matter that Jordan would never look at him in the way Brady longed for—Brady would make do with just being around him.

He'd save the other thoughts for his fantasies.

Chapter Five

WHEN it got to midday on Saturday and Jordan hadn't showed, Brady figured he'd had enough playing nurse. After all, it was the weekend, and surely Jordan had better things to do with his time than get in a cab and come to Harlem. So when his intercom buzzed and Jordan's voice came out of the speaker, Brady was momentarily stunned.

He held down the button. "Oh. Hi."

Jordan's chuckle greeted his ears. "You sound surprised. Didn't I say to expect me?"

Well, yeah, but.... Brady pushed the intercom button again. "Come on up." He held the door release button for a few seconds, thankful he was dressed this time. When he opened the door, Jordan stood there, and Brady had to hold on to the doorframe. Jordan—in jeans? Not to mention a pale blue shirt, open at the collar, with a dark blue jacket and heavy, dark brown boots.

Lord, he was beautiful. And he was holding—a picnic basket.

Brady couldn't help smiling. "Are we going… on a picnic?" Not that he could see *that* working out. He was feeling a little better, sure, but a picnic?

"We are," Jordan confirmed. "Now put on a jacket and some footwear."

"Jordan, I don't know about this. I mean, where are we going?"

Jordan grinned. "The roof."

Brady blinked. "Wait—how do *you* know about the roof?" There was a communal roof garden on top of his building, with a couple of benches, pots with flowers, and even a tree. Someone—possibly Phil— was growing tomatoes up there too. He'd had a couple during the summer, and they were delicious. Brady loved going up there. It was a regular little sun trap. He'd even managed to sneak in an hour or two of sunning himself on a towel on the weekends.

"When I was leaving last night, I ran into the building superintendent, who told me about it."

"He just… told you? Just like that?" It didn't sound like Mr. Okoru. He was an older guy who usually kept to himself.

"When he found out what I was doing here, he said a little fresh air would do you a world of good, and he showed me the roof garden. Then I got to thinking…. Today looked fair, weatherwise, so I put together something for us to eat up there." Jordan smiled. "It turns out he has a grandson your age. He was concerned because he hadn't seen you in the hallway like he usually does."

"Aw." That was nice. Brady tried to peek into the basket, but Jordan kept the lid closed. "So what are we eating?"

"Nothing if you don't put on that jacket like I told you."

Brady smirked. "Are you always this bossy?"

Jordan's eyes sparkled. "Only if I think I can get away with it. Now move it—please."

Brady laughed, grabbing his jacket from the hook behind the door. "Fine, I'm moving." Inside, he was buzzing. Jordan sure was going to a lot of trouble on his account. Then he cautioned himself not to make too big a deal out of it. *He's just looking out for me because he wants me back. That's it. Period.* This was no fairy tale, where the gorgeous boss ended up falling in love with the lowly secretary. For one thing, secretaries were usually, but not always, women—strike one—and for another, life just didn't work out like that, as much as Brady might want it to—strike two.

Brady slipped into his jacket, grabbed his keys, then paused. "Is there anything I need to bring?"

"Only you," Jordan said. "I've got everything we could need in here." He patted the lid of the basket.

Brady nodded, then stepped into his sneakers and out into the hallway, Jordan following him. Brady closed and locked the door.

Jordan cleared his throat. "Now, there are two flights of stairs to—" When Brady chuckled, Jordan rolled his eyes. "Yes, I know you *know* that, but I'm just pointing out that you have to take it slow. You haven't taken a step outside your apartment for over a week." He narrowed his gaze. "You're silently saying, 'Shut up, Jordan, and quit being a mother hen,' aren't you?"

Brady bit his lip. "The thought never crossed my mind." Jordan walked at his side as they went up the stairs, with Brady pausing at intervals to grab the rail. He shook his head. "This is ridiculous. It's only two flights, for God's sake!" He was ashamed to appear so weak and feeble.

"Put your arm around my shoulders," Jordan instructed him. Brady stared at him, and Jordan rolled his eyes. "It's the longest walk you've taken for over a week, and you're not out of the woods yet. You're going to have to take things easy for a while longer, all right? Now, put your arm around me, and lean on me if you have to."

Brady chuckled. "If I *don't* lean on you, chances are I'll fall over."

When they finally reached the door at the top of the stairs, Brady heaved a sigh of relief. He handed Jordan the key to unlock it, and Jordan held the door open for him. The fresh air that hit his face was a welcome assault, and Brady drew in a deep breath.

"Wow. So *this* is what clean air smells like."

Jordan led him to the bench, and Brady sank down onto it thankfully, leaning back against the wooden slats. Jordan sat beside him, with the basket on the ground. "This is a lovely spot."

Brady nodded, pointing to the large, heavy pot that contained a slender birch tree. "I love it when the bark peels like paper, revealing a gorgeous pinky color underneath." He sighed. "It'll start losing its leaves soon." There was definitely an autumnal nip in the air.

Jordan opened the basket and withdrew a flask and two mugs. "I thought hot coffee would be appropriate." He twisted off the cap, and the aroma filled Brady's nostrils. "And speaking of coffee... I got a bit of a shock when Celia brought me a cup."

Brady stifled a chuckle. "Oh God. Did she give you the brew from the staff room? Man, that shit is… well, shit, pardon my French. I suppose there's no accounting for taste."

Jordan groaned. "Accounting? Was that deliberate? And what taste? This is serious. I haven't had a decent cup of coffee in the office the whole time you've been off sick."

Brady knew it was wrong, but he couldn't help laughing. Fortunately, Jordan saw the funny side too. "Okay. Third drawer of my filing cabinet, that's where I keep your coffee. I've been buying that brand ever since I tasted the cra—stuff everyone else drinks. And I stash my coffee machine in my cabinet in the office. I'm not letting it get anywhere near the ones in the staff room. We could be talking contamination here." He shook his head. "No coffee since then? How on earth have you survived? Man, you must have been crankier than a barrel of monkeys."

"I thought the saying was 'more *fun* than a barrelful of monkeys,'" Jordan remarked.

"Not when you release them," Brady said darkly. He sipped the aromatic brew and sighed with pleasure. "Thank God. I can taste it. I've been off coffee since I got sick." He peered hopefully at the basket. "What other delights are you hiding in there?"

Jordan reached in and pulled out something wrapped in white paper. "It's not much, just a chicken salad wrap from the Whole Foods Market that I passed on the way here. It looks delicious. I bought one for myself too, seeing as we both need to eat healthily." He handed Brady the sandwich, smirking.

Brady smiled. "Your doctor would be proud of you." He sat in the autumn sunshine, a mug of coffee on the bench beside him, a tasty sandwich held in both hands, and a beautiful man for company.

Days don't get much better than this.

They spent about an hour up there, while Jordan related some of the week's events. By the time he'd finished, Brady was chuckling and shaking his head. "I can't leave you alone for five minutes, can I? I'd better get well ASAP, because it sounds like you need me."

For a moment Jordan was silent, and Brady wondered what he'd said to provoke such a reaction. Then Jordan sighed. "I do. Don't get me wrong—the company runs just fine without you. But *I* don't. When I called you a treasure the other day, I wasn't being facetious. I may smile at your efficiency, your organization—but that's precisely what keeps me in check. I didn't realize until this last week just how much you take out of my hands, all the little details that would otherwise clog up my schedule. And that's why I am saying—belatedly, but better late than never—thank you."

The sincerity in Jordan's voice made Brady's throat seize up, and tears pricked his eyes. "You forget. This is what you pay me for, right?" He blinked and straightened. "And if I make your life just that bit easier, then I'm doing my job." He gestured to the sandwich and the coffee. "This was… awesome. Thank you." Brady made up his mind. He would do whatever it took to get back to work as soon as he could.

"You're welcome. And I meant what I said. Take as long as you need." Jordan winked. "Now I know where the coffee is."

Brady laughed, and it was the best he'd felt for a long time.

JORDAN got out of the elevator, thankful it was Friday. The week had felt longer than usual, but maybe that was because Brady hadn't been around. Jordan hadn't seen him for a few days, but he'd kept in touch by phone. Brady sounded brighter, and that cough seemed to have finally eased off. Jordan had refrained from calling him every time he needed to know where something was or to ask about a particular meeting. Brady needed rest, not hassle.

He pushed open the doors—and stopped dead.

Brady stood there, smiling, wearing a pale blue shirt and a dark blue bow tie. He pushed his glasses back onto his nose. "Good morning, sir. The newspapers are on your desk, and here is the most important of your mail. I'll be right in with your coffee."

Delighted though he was, Jordan tempered his relief with concern. "Why are you here? Why not come in on Monday?"

Brady chuckled. "I figured it was better to come in today, to see if there was anything I could do to make my first week back start on a positive note. Less of a shock to the system that way." He grinned. "And I had to make sure you weren't about to run out of coffee."

Jordan laughed. "I *am* capable of buying my own, you know." He took the pile of envelopes. "Though it is good to have you back."

"Good to be back, sir."

Jordan walked alongside him as they headed down the hallway to his office. "You're sure you're up to this?" As wonderful as it was to see Brady, Jordan didn't want him coming back to work too early just because he knew how much Jordan relied on him.

Brady paused at the door. "It's my turn to take care of you, sir. And to that end… I've booked you in at Spiff at five o'clock."

Jordan stared at him. "Since when do I ever finish at five on a Friday?"

"Then let's make it a new rule. It's your company, sir. If anyone deserves to finish at a decent hour on a Friday, it's you."

"And the Spiff appointment?" Spiff for Men was Jordan's go-to place for haircuts, manicures, facials, and massages.

Brady's eyes gleamed. "I just thought you might be in need of a massage after the last week or so. Get Shawn to ease all the tension out of you."

Jordan shook his head as he entered Brady's office. "Shawn doesn't *do* easing—he just pummels me to death." But he couldn't deny it was a great idea. "Thank you, Brady. And I'm sure my back will thank you too—once Shawn has finished with it." He tilted his head to one side. "You ought to try it, you know. A massage is really relaxing."

Brady arched his eyebrows. "I'll take your word for it, sir. And now, if you'll excuse me, I'll get you that coffee."

Jordan left him and entered his own office, holding on to his sigh of contentment until Brady was out of earshot. *He's back.* Sanity was restored to Jordan's world. Whatever else happened, Jordan would never forget what he'd learned during the past two weeks.

Brady was worth his weight in gold.

Then it occurred to him that out of the office, Brady was a lot more relaxed, with a lot more sass. As much as he liked the efficient, polite Brady he saw every day, Jordan liked the other version even more.

Chapter Six

October

JORDAN had just finished his lunch when Brady stuck his head around the door.

"Sir? You have a call, but I wanted to see if you were done."

Jordan wiped his mouth on his napkin. "Who is it?"

"Drake Daniels. He says it's important."

Damn it. Jordan knew what that was about. "Put him through, Brady." He picked up the handset and pressed the blinking button on his phone. "Drake. Hey. I've been meaning to call you."

Drake chuckled. "Sure. I know how busy you are. But Belinda asked me this morning if you had RSVPed yet. I think she wants to know if she needs to save the guest bedroom for you. That's if you *are* coming."

"Sorry about the delay. I've been trying to get hold of Clive, my plus-one, but I haven't managed to catch him." Jordan hadn't actually made the call yet, not that Drake needed to know.

"So you are coming? Belinda will be so happy."

Drake's delighted tone poured fuel on Jordan's already guilty conscience. The invitation had been sitting on his coffee table at home for three weeks, and he hadn't done a thing about it. The party was just over a week away. *And it would be good to see Belinda and the kids.* He'd hung around with her and Drake a lot in their final year; he'd attended their wedding, stayed with them one New Year's…. The house in the Hamptons was a recent addition, however, and Jordan was curious to see it.

A weekend away from New York. A party. What was there not to like about that?

Jordan shoved aside his indecision. "Yes, I'll come. I'll let you know if I'm bringing a guest or if it'll be just me."

"Don't worry if you're coming alone. I'm pretty sure you won't stay that way for long." Drake chuckled. "In fact, I'd put money on it."

That did it. There was no way Jordan was about to let Drake fix him up, not again. He'd already been down *that* road in college, and to say it had been an unmitigated disaster was something of an understatement.

"You know what? I'm pretty certain I'll be bringing a guest, so don't make any plans on my account, okay?"

"If you say so. I'll let you get back to work. See you on the nineteenth!" Drake disconnected the call.

Jordan rested the handset in its cradle, staring off into the distance. Damn. That left him eight days. Thank God Clive was always up for a party. He was a godsend when it came to attending functions and social gatherings. And it wasn't as if they hadn't done this on several occasions already.

It had started out as a mercy mission. Jordan had attended a couple of parties and had been hit on more than once by women who wouldn't take no for an answer. Jordan had mentioned it to Clive in one of their regular phone chats, but it had been Clive's wife, Lorraine, who'd come up with the solution. She'd suggested Jordan "borrow" Clive for the evening, and Clive had jumped at the chance to go to some swanky party and play Jordan's boyfriend. Jordan didn't give a rat's ass about people knowing he was gay, not if it saved him from unwanted advances. Better to be on the receiving end of a few unwelcome glances than wandering fingers that pinched his ass.

It had worked like a charm, and after that, Clive regularly attended such functions, happy to play Jordan's attentive SO in exchange for a good night out. Lorraine loved the idea too—she got to have weekends with her girl friends, so it was a win-win for everyone concerned.

Jordan scrolled through his contacts until he found Clive, hoping not to catch him at a busy time.

After three or four rings, Clive answered. "Hey. It's been a while. How are you? Still up to your eyeballs in work?"

"Like you don't already know the answer to that one. You got a minute?"

"Sure. What's up?"

"I need my boyfriend for a weekend in the Hamptons," Jordan joked.

"Ooh, nice. You know I *love* the swanky parties. Let me check my calendar. When are we talking about?"

"Actually, it's pretty short notice. The nineteenth."

There was silence for a moment. "Of this month?"

"Yeah. I'm sorry, I know I should have called you before this, but—"

"Dude, it wouldn't have mattered if you'd called me *six months* ago. I can't do it."

"What?"

"Lorraine and I are off on a cruise to the Bahamas. All expenses paid. It's her parents' ruby wedding anniversary, and the whole family is going." Another pause. "They've been planning this for a year. Sorry."

Jordan forced a chuckle. "Look, it's not like I'm going to ask you to ditch the cruise, okay? I'm sure you'll all have a wonderful time."

"Thanks, Jordan. I'll send you a postcard. And I'm sure you'll find someone to take with you."

"Sure I will." After sending his love to Lorraine, Jordan disconnected the call and put his phone down on the desk. *Now what?* He couldn't think of a soul to invite along.

Then he realized he had more pressing problems than a plus-one. The party was eight days away, and he had nothing arranged. No travel arrangements. No car for when he got there. And then there was the packing to consider.

There was only one thing to do.

Jordan pressed the intercom. "Brady? Can you step in here, please? Bring your tablet."

Less than a minute later, Brady was sitting at Jordan's desk, his tablet on his lap. "Fire when ready."

Jordan cracked a smile. "You know, you've loosened up a little since you had the flu."

Brady blinked. "I have?"

Jordan nodded. "Not that I'm complaining, you understand." He kind of liked it. Maybe visiting Brady and taking care of him had altered their relationship a little, but it was a change for the better, as far as Jordan was concerned. "Now, I need you to make travel arrangements for me for Friday, October nineteenth, returning on the Sunday."

Brady nodded, his gaze focused on his tablet as he tapped the virtual keypad. "Yes, sir. Going where?"

"Traveling to East Hampton, by car. Anytime Friday, because I'll be taking the day off."

"Will you be driving during the weekend? Do you want to keep the chauffeur?"

"I can drive, so organize a car, please. They can drop me off at the rental place, and I'll collect it. Also, can you liaise with Donna with regards to the packing?"

"Will it be a formal weekend?"

"I don't think we're talking tuxedos, but it will be smart casual. It's a party for a friend's wedding anniversary."

Brady's fingers flew over the keypad. "Would you like me to arrange flowers and a gift to be sent?"

"That sounds perfect. For Drake and Belinda Daniels. I'll email you the address."

"One last thing. Are the travel arrangements for just you, or will you be taking a guest?"

"Unfortunately, I'll be traveling alone."

Brady jerked his head up. "Is there a problem? Can I help?"

Jordan sighed. "Only if you know someone who wants to spend a weekend in the Hamptons." When Brady's brow furrowed, Jordan explained. "My date couldn't make it."

A wistful expression stole over Brady's face. "I've seen the houses there on TV. Sort of a playground for America's rich and famous, isn't it?"

Jordan stared at him as the germ of an idea took hold. *I couldn't. It's crazy.* Then he reasoned he had nothing to lose. "Want to see it for yourself?"

"Excuse me?"

"I asked if you wanted to see it for yourself."

Brady's mouth dropped open, snapped shut, then fell open again. "You... you're serious. Why... why would you ask me?"

Jordan sighed. "Perhaps I should explain. My date who can't make it? Isn't exactly a date. He's more of an... accessory." He regarded Brady closely. "I don't talk about this at work because it has nothing to do with what goes on here, but you're not stupid. You know I'm gay, right?"

Brady nodded. "Yes, sir."

"Well, let's just say that I've received some... unwelcome advances at gatherings like this, and having a partner with me saves a lot of embarrassment all round. So... if you do decide to come with me, that would be your role."

Brady smirked, and the knot of tension in Jordan's belly dissipated. "Basically, you want me to pretend to be your boyfriend, to keep any unwanted admirers at a distance. Is that it?"

Jordan snickered. "In a nutshell. So? Will you do it?" He grinned. "Will you do your part to save your boss's ass? And I *am* being literal there."

Brady laughed at that.

Then Jordan thought clearly for a second. "Look, please don't feel you have to say yes just because it's your boss inviting you. You are perfectly free to refuse. It's just occurred to me that you might feel a little... uncomfortable in such a situation."

Brady's brow creased into a frown. "Why should it make me uncomfortable?"

"Well, pretending to be gay might not be everyone's idea of a fun weekend," Jordan joked, although his chest tightened. It had taken that thought to make him realize he really didn't want to put Brady under any pressure to do this. He genuinely liked Brady too much to cause him discomfort.

Brady stared at him for a moment, then swallowed. "And what if… I didn't have to pretend?"

Jordan couldn't account for the sudden fluttery feeling in his belly. "Oh."

Brady smiled. "Not something I talk about at work either." Then he gestured to his bow tie, cardigan, and chinos, including the pen protector in the breast pocket of his shirt. "I guess this says geek more than gay, huh?"

"Actually, now that I think about it?" Jordan chuckled. "Yeah, totally gay. Can't think why I didn't spot it sooner."

Brady snickered, and the mood lightened a little. He straightened in his chair. "As for the… invitation, my answer is yes. And no, I don't feel like you've pressured me into it. In fact, you've been very honest, and I appreciate that." He flashed Jordan a grin. "And a weekend in the Hamptons? I'd be crazy to turn that down. I may never get the chance again."

Jordan laughed. "I haven't seen Drake's house yet, so I admit to being curious too. But if you're sure?"

Brady nodded. "I'm sure. So I guess I need to make arrangements for two after all." He gazed earnestly at Jordan. "I won't let you down, sir. I'll make sure I don't embarrass you." His glance flickered downward and his smile faltered.

"What is it? What's wrong?" The change in Brady's demeanor was so abrupt that Jordan's scalp prickled.

Brady sighed. "Maybe you should find someone else."

"Why? What's changed? You were all for it a second ago."

Brady bit his lip. "I don't exactly look the part, do I? I've seen photos of you at parties and functions. I've seen the people you associate with. I... I wouldn't fit in there."

Jordan gazed at him long and hard. "What's wrong with the way you look? You're always smartly dressed. So what if you don't look like everyone else around here?" He smirked. "Have you seen the way *some* people dress? I wish they'd take a leaf out of *your* book, if I'm being totally honest."

"Thank you, but we're not talking about being in the office, are we?" Brady's earnest expression tugged at him. "The kind of people who go to weekend parties in the Hamptons wouldn't be caught dead in a cardigan and chinos." He lowered his head, his gaze focused on his tablet.

"Brady." When that got no response, Jordan softened his voice. "Brady. Look at me."

Brady raised his head, his eyes large behind those black frames.

"I like the way you look, okay? And some of the people who frequent these parties may *look* the part, but they couldn't hold a candle to you in terms of intellect *and* personality. Do you understand me?" Jordan smiled. "I like the Brady that's on the inside. What *you're* talking about is what's on the surface, and there are things we can do about that."

Brady blinked. "Such as?"

Jordan regarded him calmly. "Haircut. Manicure. New clothes." He grinned as the idea took shape in his mind. "Cinderfella, you *shall* go to the ball, and once I've finished with you, even your own mother wouldn't recognize you."

"What are you talking about?" Brady gaped at him.

"I'm talking about taking off a couple of days next week so that you and I can go shopping." Jordan cocked his head to one side. "All those times you made appointments for me to be fitted for a suit? To have a massage? Get a haircut? Well, now it's *your* turn, because all those places I usually go to? *You're* going there too."

"Are you sure I need all that?" Brady looked like a deer in headlights. "My hair's okay, isn't it?"

Jordan chuckled. "Your hair is fine. We're not talking about anything drastic, just a trim. And what's not to like about having a spa day?" He narrowed his eyes. "Have you ever *had* a spa day?" When Brady shook his head, his eyes wide, Jordan chuckled again. "Trust me. It's all part of the experience. By the time we're done, you'll not only *look* like a million dollars, you'll feel like it too."

"You said new clothes. Do I *need* new clothes?"

"We can buy something really smart for the evening of the party. The rest of the weekend should be fairly casual. Don't worry. You'll look just fine."

"If you say so, sir."

Jordan leveled a firm glance at him. "And while we're on the subject… it may be a good idea to use our little shopping spree as an opportunity to get accustomed to calling me Jordan. I don't want you calling me sir while we're there."

Brady frowned. "But.... Mr. Daniels... wasn't he at the conference in Nashville? He saw me. He'll know I'm your assistant."

Jordan shook his head. "Not when you're wearing a Tom Ford suit that fits you like a glove, and with a new sleek haircut. And so what if he does? It's none of his business." He met Brady's anxious gaze head-on. "Still want to do this?"

Brady said nothing for a moment, his hands restless on his lap. Then slowly he lifted his chin and looked Jordan in the eye. "Yes, sir—I mean, Jordan."

Jordan beamed at him. "That's my Brady. Okay, you go ahead with the travel arrangements. We can talk about the *other* arrangements once they're in place."

Brady nodded and got to his feet. "I'll get right on it." He left the office, pulling the door shut behind him.

Jordan stared at the closed door, his mind in a whirl. It still struck him as a crazy idea, but he couldn't help the ripple of anticipation that trickled through him. He couldn't wait to see the finished product.

It was then that the realization hit home.

He was happy Brady was going with him.

A second later Brady's words finally sank in. *And he's gay.* Not that it made a difference. *So what? It's not as if I'm going to look at him in a whole new light—am I?*

It surprised Jordan to find out he wasn't quite sure.

BRADY sank into his chair and stared blankly at his monitor. A weekend... in the Hamptons. With Jordan.

It didn't seem real.

Then he thought about Jordan's plans to give him what amounted to a makeover. Brady wasn't sure how he felt about that part. Always sensitive to his appearance, Brady did his best to blend into the background, and from the sound of it, that wasn't what Jordan had in mind at all.

How do I feel about that? Maybe it wouldn't be so bad. Some new clothes, his hair trimmed, a manicure....

The last thing he wanted was to let Jordan down.

It was so difficult to clear his thoughts when inside his head was a tangled mess of practicality and emotion, logic and lust. Well, not really *lust*. If he'd been crushing on Jordan before he'd gone down with the flu, it was ten times worse after. He'd seen another side to his boss, and he'd really liked what he saw.

The irony of the whole situation.... To pretend to be Jordan's boyfriend, to act like he was in love with him....

Brady didn't think *that* part of the charade would prove taxing. Not in the slightest.

Chapter Seven

BRADY got out of the car and stared up at the building in front of him.

Jordan spoke with the driver, then joined Brady as the car pulled away. He nudged Brady's arm. "It's just a store."

Brady gaped at him. "How can you say that? It's *Tom Ford*, for God's sake. He's up there with Prada, and Jimmy Choo, and Christian Louboutin." He drew in a deep breath. "I'm sorry. I'm just not used to shopping for a suit on Madison Avenue, I guess. Especially not from a designer who I've only read about and seen on TV."

Jordan's hand was at his back, and Brady took some comfort from that. "Listen. We're going to walk in there, browse through the ready-to-wear suits, and if we're *really* lucky, we'll find something off the rack that fits you perfectly. If not, that's why we came here first. These guys are geniuses. They'll rustle you up a suit that *will* fit you perfectly, and in time for next weekend." He smiled. "Now… ready to go inside?"

Brady laid a hand on his arm. "Just one thing. You said it will be smart casual. Do I really need a *suit*? I mean, couldn't we go in for something a little more… low-key?"

Jordan's smile lit up his face. "I think we can go with that. Let's look around first, okay?"

Brady nodded happily. He could deal with that.

Jordan pushed open the door, and Brady found himself in the menswear department. For a moment he had to stop and stare, because it wasn't what he'd expected at all. The first thing that caught his attention was an eye-catching fuchsia ribbed sweater.

"Wow. That's… bright."

Jordan snickered. "I guess I picked the wrong day to leave my shades in the office."

Brady wandered over to the glass table full of neatly folded sweaters and stroked the fabric. Then he saw the price tag, and his jaw dropped. "Jordan…. Jordan!"

"What's wrong?"

Brady just stared at him, openmouthed, pointing to the label. "It's… nearly nine hundred dollars."

Jordan grinned. "Relax. You don't need a nine-hundred-dollar sweater, especially one that could light up a room." He peered at the sweater. "Well, it *is* cashmere, after all."

Brady snorted. "At that price I'd expect nothing less than gold."

Jordan laughed. "Go take a look around. I'm searching for something to wear too."

That made Brady feel better. He caught sight of a row of jackets and went to take a closer look. No sooner had he reached it than a young man approached, dressed in black, with beautifully sculpted eyebrows.

"Looking for something in particular? Can I help?"

Brady gave him a polite smile. "Thanks, but I'm just going to look around until something grabs my interest."

The young man nodded. "I'll be right over there if you need me." He glided across the floor to another customer.

Brady went back to the racks, smiling at a camouflage jacket done in velvet—until he saw its price tag: $4,050. Who would wear a *velvet* camo jacket? And at that price? Then his smile widened when he saw a mannequin wearing a funnel-neck cardigan in black. *That's more like it.* Brady fingered the soft fabric, now recognizing it as cashmere. He gave the price tag a cursory glance, not really surprised at this point to see it was more than $2,000. He was starting to believe they could wrap a half-eaten donut in cashmere and price it at a thousand bucks and someone would buy it.

"That would really suit you." The sales assistant was back, nodding, those eyebrows arched.

Before Brady could utter a word, Jordan called out his name. He glanced across the store to where Jordan stood in front of a rack of casual jackets, beckoning him and smiling. He held up a dark brown leather biker jacket with one long zipper that went diagonally and three smaller ones, also diagonal.

"What do you think?"

Brady touched the soft leather and fell in love. "Oh wow."

Jordan held it against him, nodding. "Try it on. And don't look at the price tag. That's an order."

Brady bit back his smirk. He removed his own plain black jacket and slipped his arms into the leather sleeves. Unhurriedly, he pulled up the zipper. It fit him as though it had been made for him.

"Oh. Oh, this is… beautiful."

Jordan nodded. "It really suits you." He helped Brady out of it and returned it to its hanger. "I think I'm going to keep hold of this one. And I also think a pair of straight-fit black jeans would complement it perfectly."

"Jeans? Really?"

Jordan grinned. "What did I say? Trust me."

That was when Brady really relaxed. There remained one little niggle, however.

"Jordan, it's not that I don't appreciate you bringing me here, but…." He gestured to the gorgeous clothing around them. "This isn't exactly cheap. You can't spend all that money on me."

Jordan put down the jacket and placed his hands on Brady's shoulders. "One—you are doing me a huge favor by accompanying me. Two—think of it as a bonus."

"Huh?"

Jordan's dark eyes were kind. "You do so much for me—and *don't* say that's your job. We both know you go above and beyond your job description on a daily basis. This is small recompense for everything you do. And three—I want to do it." He smiled. "It will make me happy."

Brady's chest tightened. "Far be it from me to come between you and happiness." Then he tried to sneak a peek at the price tag.

Jordan wagged his finger. "Uh-uh. That's for my eyes only. All you get to do is choose a few more outfits."

Not that the shopping expedition went without a few hiccups. When Brady cast longing glances at the Prince of Wales classic-fit shirt, Jordan steered him firmly but gently toward the gray sharkskin tailored shirt or the classic-fit shirt in fine pink poplin. When they got to cardigans, Jordan didn't even let him get close enough to breathe on them. Brady merely sighed and followed him. But he had to admit, the slim-fit evening shirt in white silk Jordan picked out for him was... gorgeous.

And when Jordan found him the dark green cocktail jacket and black pants—and a matching bow tie—Brady was officially in heaven. The outfit was so... *him*, and yet it wasn't. It belonged to a more elegant Brady, a Brady who wouldn't look out of place in a roomful of equally elegant party guests. He absolutely loved it, even when Jordan mentioned how the wool jacket might prove a little... warm for the Hamptons in October. Brady would not be swayed, saying he could always take it off. Jordan gave up at that point.

The sales assistant clung to Brady like a shadow, so obviously that Jordan leaned in close to whisper, "Either he thinks you're about to steal something, or he wants to give you his number."

Brady snickered. "Like I'd want *his* number."

"What's wrong with him?" Jordan gazed across the store to where the young man was watching them. "He seems okay."

"If you like pretty boys. Not my type."

Jordan chuckled. "You have a type? Do tell."

It took all of Brady's strength not to say he liked older guys with dark eyes, a permanent five-o'clock shadow, and strong, broad shoulders. Instead he coughed. "Yeah—anything except pretty boys."

When they finally left the store, with Brady clutching three or four bags of clothing, he was giddy with excitement. Like a little kid, he wanted to go home and try on everything—hardly the behavior of a mature twenty-seven-year-old.

But Brady didn't feel twenty-seven. He felt like he was eighteen again, about to go to the prom and longing to dance with Chase Garton, who was without doubt the most good-looking boy in his high school—and who never even looked at him once.

At least Jordan will be paying attention to me. Not that Brady expected anything to come of it. *Not a fairy tale, remember?*

Jordan got off the phone to the car service. "He'll be here in about ten minutes."

"We're done now, right?"

Jordan shook his head slowly. "Shoes."

"Shoes?"

"Shoes," Jordan repeated in a firm tone.

Brady indicated the store behind them with a flick of his head. "We couldn't have gotten them in there?"

Another shake of the head. "We're going to Christopher Street. And before we get there, you're not allowed to look at price tags in there either."

Brady rolled his eyes. "Let me guess. The shoes are all made from the skin of some rare mountain goat that can only be located in the Himalayas."

Jordan widened his eyes. "How did you know?" When Brady gasped, he snorted. "Gotcha. We're going to Leffot. I buy all my shoes from there."

By then Brady knew it was pointless to argue. "I shudder to think how much you just paid for all this."

Jordan shrugged. "I look at it this way. I don't have any hobbies, expensive or otherwise. I go on vacation once a year. So what if I want to spend my money on clothes that make me feel good?" He smiled. "And you too, in this instance. Because you did feel good in that jacket and shirt, didn't you?"

Brady couldn't deny that.

Jordan nodded again. "And just in case you think I'm being extravagant... Leffot has a selection of 'preowned' shoes. Their own brand, but ones clients have sold back to them, in excellent condition. That's if you don't mind the idea of secondhand shoes."

Brady laughed. "Yeah, right. Secondhand *designer* shoes. I think they'd be a step up from the ones you'd find in Goodwill, right?"

Jordan snickered. "Okay, a fair point. But when we've finished shoe shopping, that will be it for the day. And seeing as we won't be all that far from one of my favorite little Italian restaurants, I thought we might have dinner." He tilted his head. "That is, if you don't mind Italian?"

Brady beamed. "I love Italian. And dinner sounds great. Thank you." Inside he was buzzing. The day was shaping up to be one of the best he'd ever had, and the prospect of dinner with Jordan made it just about perfect.

"Though I should warn you," Jordan added. "Palma isn't exactly huge. It's a cozy place, and the food is awesome."

A cozy Italian restaurant. *Someone up there must really like me.* Then Brady thought about how much money Jordan had already spent. "On one condition. I buy dinner." When Jordan opened his mouth, no doubt to protest, Brady shook his head. "No deal. Either I buy dinner—or no designer shoes, preowned or otherwise."

Jordan sighed. "Fine. You can pay for dinner." He stroked his chin. "There's always McDonald's on West Third Street...."

Brady rolled his eyes. "Oh, look, Jordan made a funny. Don't even joke about it. Not after you have me drooling at the thought of Italian food. And I'm good for it, after all." He gave Jordan a hard stare. "A pretty good meal, I can deal with. Buying my clothes at Tom Ford? Yeah, not so much, unless it's one piece at a time on credit."

Jordan chuckled. "Just teasing." He patted Brady's arm. "You'll love it."

Brady was pretty certain that if Jordan was involved, loving it would not be a problem.

Trying not to get his hopes up, on the other hand….

Brady was going to have to be very careful. Because there was the very real possibility that Jordan could break his heart.

Chapter Eight

BRADY had to admit, Palma was a real find. It didn't look like much on the outside—three slim bifold windows, their frames painted in a creamy yellow—but inside, it was a delight. To one side there was a long wood-topped bar with stools, and at the far end of the bar stood a large earthenware pot, containing what looked like a small tree. To the other side were wooden tables covered in silverware and glasses, with candles glowing. Jordan had been correct: the interior wasn't all that big, but Jordan told him there were more tables out the back, with a covering in case of inclement weather.

Aromas assaulted him as they entered, making Brady's mouth water. "If the food tastes as good as it smells, this is going to be fantastic." He gave Jordan a quick smile. "This was a really good idea." Inside his head was an insistent voice that kept repeating, *Don't be stupid. It's just dinner. It's not a date. Don't make it out to be more than it is. Don't get carried away. It's not a date. It's not a—*

Jordan cleared his throat. "Brady?"

With a start Brady realized the server was waiting patiently to show them to a table.

Jordan's eyes sparkled. "You did want to eat, right?"

Brady rolled his eyes. "No, I thought we'd come here to admire the decor." He smirked.

As they followed the server, Brady did his utmost to breathe evenly. If he wasn't careful, he'd do something stupid, and then Jordan would regret asking him to spend the weekend in the Hamptons. That still felt so unreal. Then he glanced down at his shopping bags.

Definitely *not* a dream.

AFTER watching Brady read through the menu at least four times, Jordan figured he had to step in. "Problems?"

Brady looked up, biting his lip. "Too many delicious-sounding things on here to choose from. I think I need a little help. Got any suggestions?" He smiled. "I mean, seeing as you come here pretty regularly."

Jordan knew that feeling all too well. "Seeing as it's your first time, let's go for the whole experience. Antipasti, a couple more courses, dessert...."

Brady snickered. "Then our next stop will be a tailor's to let out the clothes you just bought. Because if I eat that much.... Trust me, I could put on ten pounds just by reading this menu."

Jordan gave him an appreciative glance. Brady was slim, obviously careful about what he ate. Then it struck him that until recently, he hadn't paid any attention to how Brady looked. He was just…. Brady. It had taken him being off sick to open Jordan's eyes.

"Jordan?" Brady was grinning at him. "You did want to eat, right?"

"Very funny." Jordan scanned the menu, then came to a decision. "How about if I choose for both of us, and then you get to try mine too? I recall *someone* saying he was a regular little omnivore, so I'm assuming there's nothing I need to avoid ordering."

"You'd assume correctly—although this might be a good moment to point out that I have little experience with tentacles, in case you were thinking of ordering something a little more… exotic." Brady's eyes sparkled behind his glasses.

"I take it calamari wouldn't be too exotic for you?"

Brady chuckled. "Calamari, fine. Octopus, yeah, not so much." He shivered. "Too many legs."

Jordan cleared his throat. "Can I just point out here that squid have the same number of legs as an octopus? Even if they do have two additional suckerless tentacles for feeding with."

Brady stared at him. "Oh my. I'm having dinner with a marine biologist." He rolled his eyes.

Jordan had a feeling dinner would prove to be entertaining.

The server appeared at their table, and Jordan rattled off his selection, along with a bottle of Ros Alba. Then he leaned back in his seat and regarded Brady inquiringly. "So, tell me about Brady Donovan."

"What would you like to know that you haven't already seen on my résumé?" Brady appeared relaxed, which pleased Jordan. This had been an impulse, but once he'd thought about it, dinner was a great opportunity to get to know the man who'd be keeping him company the following weekend.

"What made you decide to follow this particular career?"

Brady snickered. "If you ask my mom, she'd say I was born to it. She used to regale all her visitors and relations with tales of how I color-coordinated my closet."

"Lots of people do that," Jordan remonstrated.

"Not when they're four years old, they don't. And then there were the times we went on vacation, and I'd draw up an itinerary of what we'd be doing and when." Brady shook his head. "*Other* guys' moms show prospective boyfriends their baby photos—*mine* got told embarrassing stories of how really anal I was."

"You shouldn't be embarrassed," Jordan said quietly. "You're amazing at what you do." He cleared his throat as the server approached their table, carrying an ice bucket with a bottle of wine sitting in it. Once Jordan had tasted it and the server poured two glasses, Jordan raised his. "To you, Brady. The most efficient, capable personal assistant it has been my pleasure to know."

Brady stared at him for a moment before taking a sip of wine. "Can I ask you something about today?"

"Sure." Brady's slightly cautious manner had him curious.

"I know you said I should consider the clothes a reward for all I do, but this whole makeover so that even my mom wouldn't recognize me…. That *was* what you said, right? Well, I just got to thinking… I'm not sure I'd want that. It's like… you're trying to change me. So I suppose that got me wondering…. Do I *need* changing?"

Shit. Jordan put down his glass. "Listen to me," he said in a low voice, leaning forward and taking Brady's hand in his. "No one is trying to change you. *You* were the one who said you didn't want to embarrass me, not that you ever could. The new clothes are simply to make you feel good. That's why I only bought things you were happy with. If you'd wanted that velvet camo jacket, I wouldn't have batted an eyelid." He smiled. "I *might* have lifted an eyebrow if you'd wanted that bright pink sweater, however...." Jordan lightly squeezed Brady's hand. "I only wanted you to go to this weekend feeling confident. And if you want to go in your chinos, white shirt, cardigan, and bow tie, that's fine by me too." He released Brady's fingers.

Brady shuddered out a sigh. "Thank you. That makes me feel a whole lot better." He took off his glasses and rubbed the bridge of his nose.

"Are they irritating you?"

Brady shook his head. "They rub sometimes. I really need to get used to my contacts. I have boxes of them, sitting on my bathroom shelf." He lifted his head and smiled, and the breath caught in Jordan's throat at the sight. Brady's eyes were beautiful, a deep rich brown that was almost bronze, framed with long dark lashes.

It wasn't his place to express an opinion, but Jordan secretly hoped Brady would get used to his contacts too. Then he reasoned that looking into those eyes on a frequent basis would prove a terrible distraction.

The more time I spend around him, the more I notice that he's a beautiful man. A gorgeous man, whose personality matched his exterior.

IS that how he sees me? Efficient? Capable? Then Brady scolded himself for expecting anything else. This was his *boss*, for God's sake. The whole shopping trip had gotten his head in a mess. Brady had thought he had a handle on things, and then Jordan totally derailed all such thoughts by holding his goddamn *hand*. He took a drink of wine and forced himself to be rational.

This is just dinner. Then I go home, and by Monday everything will be back to normal.

Except Brady had no clue what was normal anymore. And since when was it normal to go to a weekend party in the Hamptons?

Thankfully, the antipasti arrived, and Brady shoved aside such reflections in favor of *prosciutto di Parma*, *mozzarella di bufala*, and the most delicious focaccia he'd ever tasted. The fried calamari melted in his mouth, so unlike the chewy, almost rubberlike examples he'd tried in the past. He was sure his face was nothing but one blissful smile from the first bite to the last.

When the server took away their dishes, Brady let loose a happy sigh. "Now I know why you like eating here."

"I gather you like olives," Jordan remarked dryly.

It took Brady a second or two to register his words, and then his mouth fell open. "Oh my God. I ate most of them, didn't I?"

Jordan chuckled. "You let me have one or two, yes." He smirked. "I'm hoping to be luckier with the pasta."

Brady's cheeks grew hot, until he spied the twinkle in Jordan's eyes. He straightened in his chair and lifted his chin high. "You obviously need to be quicker off the mark."

Jordan laughed. "My plan was to distract you with a cute server. I figured it was the only way I stood a chance of eating anything tonight."

Brady was glad he wasn't eating the next course at that moment. Spraying one's boss with half-chewed pasta wasn't the way to impress.

The two pasta dishes arrived, and Brady had to admit, the taste of prosciutto-filled tortellini and spinach-and-ricotta-filled agnolotti was sublime. The tomato and basil sauce was the perfect accompaniment, and Brady used his last morsel of focaccia to wipe up every last smear.

Jordan grinned. "Hmm. Maybe you were right. I do have the number of a good tailor."

Brady brandished his focaccia. "This is all your fault. If you bring me to amazing restaurants where the food is nothing short of awesome, what do you expect?" He popped the bread into his mouth and savored its flavor before taking another sip of wine. "And this is delicious." He sank back into his chair, perfectly content.

"Anything else I should know about you? Apart from your early penchant for color coordination," Jordan added with a smile. "Do you come from a large family?" When Brady blinked, Jordan gave an embarrassed shrug. "I'm amazed at how little I know about you after three years of working together."

"Quite the opposite." Brady poured out the wine, refilling their glasses. "There's just me, my mom, and my dad. They live in Florida."

Jordan widened his eyes. "I'd have thought you would prefer to live there. New York can be pretty harsh in winter."

Brady snickered. "Excuse me? What temperatures did we get this past June? Ninety-five degrees? For God's sake, the asphalt was melting on my shoes. And I *chose* to come work in New York. Florida may have a great climate, but to be honest, it's also dull as dishwater, not to mention as flat as a pancake."

"And, of course, New York City is famous for its hills and valleys," Jordan interjected.

Brady's eyes sparkled. "There's *always* something going on here. And I'm not just talking arts and culture. If I want to get a bit closer to nature, all I have to do is walk a block and I'm in Harlem Meer." He cocked his head to one side. "Have you ever been there?" When Jordan shook his head, Brady sighed. "It's beautiful, especially now when the colors are changing. I love walking along the shoreline, watching the birds on the island, the reflections of the trees in the water…." It was also a romantic place, where Brady had often dreamed of walking hand in hand with someone special, leaning his head on their shoulder, a strong arm around his waist.

A wonderful fantasy.

All such thoughts were driven away by the arrival of pan-roasted chicken, redolent with the aroma of lemon and garlic, and pan-seared salmon with sautéed spinach. Jordan made sure Brady got to taste the salmon, and Brady made equally sure that a piece of chicken ended up on Jordan's plate. By the time he'd eaten the last mouthful, Brady had begun to reconsider the idea of dessert. It was only Jordan's promise that the affogato was worth it that made him relent.

The vanilla gelato drowned in espresso turned out to be every bit as wonderful as Jordan had promised, and Brady helped himself to the last spoonful with another sigh of contentment.

"Okay, you were right. That was amazing. Thank you."

Jordan split the final bit of wine between their glasses, then leaned back, smiling. "I should be thanking you. After all, you're paying for it, right?"

"That was the deal." Brady estimated the bill would be at least one hundred fifty dollars, but if that was what three courses of heaven tasted like, it was *so* worth it. He patted his belly. "They don't expect to have us out of here right this second, do they? Because I'm not sure I could move right now." Then he opened his eyes wide. "Oh God. Tell me they're not going to bring coffee. I don't think I have the space for that."

Jordan laughed softly. "Actually? Italians don't end a meal with a large frothy cappuccino. An espresso, maybe, but we already had that. I was thinking more along the lines of a small *limoncello*. It's a liqueur made from lemons, and it's strong but delicious." He peered at Brady. "Do you want to try it?"

Brady nodded, unable to stop himself. For some reason he was finding it increasingly difficult to say no to Jordan. It seemed to be the pattern for the day.

When the tiny glasses arrived, filled with a hazy lemon liquid, Brady took a tentative sip, and the alcohol warmed him instantly. Definitely something to be savored slowly. Then he realized he had another reason for taking his time—he didn't want the day to finally come to an end.

But all too soon, Jordan was calling for a car to pick them up, and Brady's bliss vanished with the last drops of limoncello. He said nothing as the car drove through the streets of Manhattan, heading for Harlem—Jordan had insisted on dropping him at his apartment, along with all his shopping bags. Jordan was equally quiet, but the silence wasn't uncomfortable. Brady wanted to find the words to fully express what a great day he'd had, but for some reason, they wouldn't come. Maybe that was a good thing. Brady had a feeling that if he opened his mouth, he'd spill more than he wanted to.

"Is everything in place for next Friday?" Jordan asked as the car pulled up outside the building.

Brady nodded. "It'll take just under two and a half hours by car to get to East Hampton, three if we hit traffic, and there'll be a rental car waiting for us. I've arranged for us to leave at noon, unless you'd like to get there later?"

Jordan shook his head. "No, that sounds perfect. It'll give us time to acclimatize before the evening." He met Brady's gaze. "Have a good weekend. I'll see you Monday morning." Then he smiled, and it reached his eyes. "Thank you for your company today. Of course, we still have one more excursion before next Friday."

Brady frowned. "We do?"

Jordan grinned. "You're going to love your spa day. You'll be so relaxed at the end of it, we'll have to pour you into the car." His eyes gleamed in the car's interior light. "My only regret is I don't get to watch you on the receiving end of Shawn or Dominic's enthusiastic massage."

Brady climbed out of the car, clutching his bags. His only thought as he watched the car pull away was that a massage kind of implied skin. A lot of skin. On display. Then he recalled Jordan's words, and he breathed a sigh of relief. *He won't get to see me.*

There was a downside to that, however. Brady wouldn't get to see Jordan either.

What I wouldn't give to be in that room….

Jordan, lying facedown on a massage table, with only a folded towel covering that firm ass.

Down, boy. Thinking about his boss's ass was *not* a good thing.

Danger, Will Robinson!

Chapter Nine

AS soon as Jordan clicked his voicemail and heard his mother's dulcet tones, he knew what was coming. It had to have been a couple of months since he'd paid his parents a visit, and his mother's polite inquiry was her way of saying he was long overdue. A glance at his phone told him it wasn't too late for a call.

"You *are* alive. I'll cancel the obituary in the *New York Times*."

Jordan chuckled. "We've talked about your experiments with sarcasm. It really isn't you." He sighed. "You can't have it both ways, you know. You can't make comments about me running a little empire and then expect me to—"

"To what? Come see your parents once in a while? Of course, Westchester County is *so* very far from the

Upper East Side, isn't it? I mean, it must take you all of *fifty minutes* to reach us by car."

"And again with the sarcasm." Not to mention she had no idea how bad the traffic was.

"Jordan." Her voice softened. "We haven't seen you for nine weeks. I know it's short notice, but would it be such an imposition to come for dinner tomorrow evening? Fiona will be here, and she's bringing a guest. I thought it would be pleasant to spend some time together. Unless you'd rather come next weekend?"

"That won't be possible. I'm away next weekend." Jordan considered the idea. If Fi was bringing a guest, his mother might be less inclined to focus on her usual topic of conversation, which was Jordan's lack of a partner. In fact, that could work to his advantage. "Okay, I'll be there."

"Oh, wonderful. We'll expect you at some point tomorrow afternoon. Your father made some noises about having a barbecue, but that will depend entirely on the weather. And if you want to stay the night instead of heading back to the city, you'd be more than welcome. You haven't done that for so long."

"Who's Fiona bringing, by the way?" Jordan was dying of curiosity. It wasn't like his sister to do such a thing.

"Oh, some friend of hers—a coworker, I believe. Well, I'd better make sure everything's ready for tomorrow." She paused, and Jordan couldn't miss the warmth that crept into her voice. "It will be *so* good to see you." She disconnected the call.

Her obvious pleasure made him glad he'd said yes. It was only as he was getting into bed a couple of hours later that a thought occurred to him. He'd assumed Fi's friend was someone she was interested in, but then a horrible suspicion began to filter through his brain.

What if Fi was bringing someone to meet *him*?

Jordan knew his mother could be sneaky when she put her mind to it. He wouldn't put it past her or Fiona to concoct this scheme simply as a means of introducing Jordan to some eligible bachelor. Then he shook his head, appalled that he could even countenance such a supposition.

They wouldn't—would they? He snorted. Of *course* they would. Doubtless his mother's primary concern was future grandchildren—there had been several not-so-subtle hints in the past already—but any way she dressed it up, she wanted him settled down and married.

Jordan stared at the ceiling. It wasn't that he was opposed to the idea of marriage; it was simply a case of a lack of opportunity, of suitable guys whose whole focus wasn't to make him spend more time with them and less with his company, or of finding that one person where the connection and chemistry were so unmistakable that they both heard the click.

Let's face it. The only guy I've really noticed lately has been Brady. A guy who until recently had almost melted into the background.

Except I'm seeing him now, aren't I?

Something uncoiled deep in Jordan's belly, and it wasn't an unpleasant sensation. *I sure am.*

BY ten o'clock the following morning, Jordan was starting to regret his decision. They'd been down this road before. His mother had tried on more than one occasion—unsuccessfully—to fix him up with a guy, and Jordan had really thought she'd learned her lesson. Why she didn't apply herself equally to finding Fi a husband, Jordan wasn't quite sure, but then Fiona always seemed to have some guy or other in tow. She was smart, however—she didn't bring them anywhere near their mother.

I suppose I should be grateful to have parents who accept me, who want to see me settled and happy. Not that Jordan didn't want that too—it was just proving a little difficult to bring about.

When his phone rang and Brady's name flashed up on the screen, Jordan smiled. "Hey."

"Jordan, we have a problem." Brady sounded flustered, and that was enough to send a wave of panic through him. Brady *never* sounded flustered.

"What's up?"

"I'm at the office. I've been here for the last two hours. I'm sorry to call you on the weekend, but I've been trying to fix this and I'm getting nowhere."

"Okay, calm down. What's wrong?"

He caught Brady's deep intake of breath. "I was catching up on work from yesterday, just checking that everything had gone smoothly while we were out shopping. Do you recall how we were about to take on a contract with a new company to cover employees' insurance? Remember? We found a better deal?"

"*You* found a better deal, if I remember correctly. Yeah, sure."

"Well, I got an email from them. The switchover was supposed to be this weekend, only… they're asking why we haven't deposited the funds with them, as we agreed. That should have happened yesterday."

"Have you called the bank?"

Brady let out an exasperated sigh. "First thing I did when I saw the email. The bank says they haven't received any transfer of funds from us for that account. So I'm sitting here, going over everything…. Jordan, the money went out from our account, right on time.

The trouble is, I have no clue where it went. If the bank doesn't have it, then where the hell is it?"

"Have you called Bryan in Finance?"

"Yes, and I think I pissed him off. He obviously didn't appreciate an early call on a Saturday."

Jordan suppressed a growl. "Well, tough. This is his job. He should be dealing with this." He got to his feet. "I'm going to call a cab. I'll be there as fast as I can, all right? Put the coffee on. Sounds like we're going to need it. And Brady? Thanks for trying to sort this. Don't worry. We'll work it out." He disconnected the call, then found the number for a taxi, his mind buzzing.

What the hell?

Jordan wasn't too concerned about the missing funds—money had a habit of turning up eventually— but he didn't like the idea of Brady getting stressed out about this, not when it should be someone else's headache. And when all the dust had settled, *someone's* ass was going to get well and truly kicked.

Jordan walked into his office and found Brady sitting on the carpet, surrounded by printouts and peering at a laptop. "Still no luck?"

Brady glanced up and shook his head. "This makes no sense. I've checked and double-checked. All the paperwork was in order, the debits set up.... It all went like clockwork at our end, so why isn't the money where it should be?"

Jordan walked over to the coffeepot, poured two mugs, then handed one to Brady. He squatted on the carpet next to him. "Okay, let's be logical here. The money has been taken from our account, right?"

"Right." Brady sipped his coffee.

"And our records show the bank taking the money?"

"Yes, but they said—"

Jordan shook his head. "I don't care what they said. This is their problem, and they are going to sort it out. Who did you speak with at the bank?"

Brady reached for his pad of Post-its. "Trey Layton, a clerk in their Business section."

Jordan smiled. "Then maybe it's time to go over Trey's head. With a company this size, I want to speak to someone who knows what they're talking about. Get the bank on the phone, please. This time, *I'll* take the call."

Brady gave a tired grin. "That might work. They weren't intimidated by me, that's for sure." He got up off the floor, went to his desk, and tapped out a number on the keypad. Then he held out the handset. "Give 'em hell, boss."

Jordan took it and began talking. It didn't take long before the guy on the other end was remonstrating loudly that it had nothing to do with them, that the funds weren't showing in the account.

"Then I suggest you get someone to check again, because if this isn't dealt with to my satisfaction, I will be taking my business elsewhere. I'm sure there are plenty of banks in the city who would *love* to have Jordan Wolf Accounting on their books. You might want to think about that before you call me back." He hung up.

Brady laughed. "See, I can't do that. I'm just a lowly PA. *My* threats cut no ice."

Jordan arched his eyebrows. "There is *nothing* about you that is lowly. So let's put all this paperwork back where it belongs and wait for them to get their heads out of their asses."

"You don't want to take a look? Check to see if I've missed something?"

Jordan smiled. "I trust your judgment. If you say the mistake isn't ours, I believe you. No, this is the bank's mess. They can clear it up. Because if they don't, I will raise one hell of a stink in the business community." He got up, and they began filing papers into folders.

Jordan had just poured himself another coffee when the phone rang. He grinned at Brady. "Showtime."

BRADY loved watching Jordan in full-on boss mode. The man was impressive, speaking coolly, calmly, with a patience Brady envied right then. When a huge smile broke out over Jordan's face, Brady knew it was all over.

"Thank you, Mr. Devon. I appreciate the call." Jordan disconnected, replaced the handset, then grinned at Brady. "Well, what do you know? It seems there was a banking error, something to do with their computer system. Miraculously, our funds have suddenly made an appearance and are where they should be."

"A banking error?" Brady gaped at him. "So what was this, 'we didn't get the transfer of funds' crap?"

"That's just standard operating procedure for business—never admit you've made a mistake. Amazing what happens when you get to speak to the president of the bank, isn't it? Mr. Devon assures me it was just a computer glitch." Jordan's eyes gleamed. "Apparently Trey called him at home, which didn't go down too well. I imagine Trey will be in a world of shit come Monday morning."

Brady got on his laptop. "I'll email the insurance company to let them know what's going on. At least all our employees are covered." He heaved a sigh of relief. "Thank you. I was going out of my mind. Sorry to ruin your Saturday morning."

Jordan sighed. "My Saturday was already ruined last night."

Brady paused in the middle of typing. "But I thought last night was great?" He'd loved every minute of it. For a moment his heart plummeted.

Jordan groaned. "Oh God, I'm sorry. No, believe me, last night *was* great, right up until the moment when my mom invited me to dinner this evening."

"What's so awful about dinner?"

"Nothing—until you factor in my mom and sister colluding to set me up with some guy."

Brady grinned. "Aw. Seriously?" Did families still do that? Thank God *his* parents had never tried. Sure, they dropped hints on a regular basis, such as asking when he was going to settle down, when he was going to bring someone special to meet them, and so on. He figured his mom knew what would happen if she tried to fix him up with someone.

There would be Words.

"Well, I'm pretty certain that's what they're doing. It wouldn't be the first time. And this is *not* funny."

Brady hastily straightened his features.

Just then Jordan's phone pinged, and he peered at the screen. His face fell as he shoved the phone into his jeans pocket. "Sometimes I hate being right." He shook his head. "A text from my sister, telling me she can't wait for me to meet her coworker, Corbin. She's sure I'll 'just love him,'" he said, air-quoting.

The thought made Brady's stomach clench. He knew it was stupid, but the idea of Jordan meeting Corbin's gaze across a room….

I really do have it bad, don't I?

Then it struck him that Jordan had grown silent. Brady regarded him in concern. Jordan was staring at him, a familiar twinkle in his eyes.

"Brady, would you do me a really big favor?"

Brady lifted his eyebrows. "I thought I was doing that next weekend. The Hamptons? Pretending to be your SO? Fending off the advances of all those rich women who want to—"

"Yeah, I know, but I've just had an idea how to derail my mom and sister with one easy move. Only, I'd need your help."

Brady suddenly saw the light. "You want me... to go to your parents' place for dinner this evening, don't you? But what good will that do? You said your sister is bringing a coworker—that's all *I'd* be, right?" Then he stilled. "Wait a minute. You don't want to take me as a colleague, do you?"

Jordan held up his hands. "Nothing heavy, I swear. I'd maybe hold your hand at the table, give you a few lingering glances...."

"And you don't foresee problems with this... subterfuge? Such as, your mom thinking you're dating me?" Not that Brady had any objections to such a plan.

Jordan shrugged. "It's not like I'm about to tell her we're engaged, right? You'd just be my current boyfriend. And besides...." He grinned. "I'm trying to picture her expression when I turn up with you." He tilted his head to one side. "I held your hand at dinner last night and it didn't seem to freak you out. Granted, those were different circumstances, but it's just for one evening. You'd be buying me some breathing space, that's all." He smiled. "Think of it as practice for the Hamptons."

Brady was severely torn. On the one hand, the idea of cozying up with Jordan for an evening was very pleasant, even if it was only make-believe. But on the other, having him so close, living out Brady's fantasy....

Then he gave himself a swift mental kick. *More time spent with Jordan? Being close to him?*

Like he'd turn *that* down.

"Luckily for you, my social calendar is empty this evening." Brady gave a slow nod. "Okay. I'll do it. Let me know what time you want me to be ready, and give me an idea of what to wear."

Jordan smiled. "Could you organize a car to pick me up at three thirty, and then we'll come get you? And wear whatever you feel comfortable in." He stroked his chin. "My mom mentioned spending the night there, but I think it would cause fewer problems if we didn't. We'll take a taxi back to the city."

"Fine." Brady considered Jordan's clothing suggestion. "As for wearing what's comfortable, I know where your mom lives, remember? I sent her flowers? Somehow I don't think my favorite jeans and a tee would go down so well in Westchester. Don't worry, I won't embarrass you."

Jordan's frank gaze sent shivers down his spine. "I never thought you would." He glanced at the phone on Brady's desk. "You'd better call the car service ASAP. Then we'll get out of here." He flashed Brady a grin. "We have to get ready for this evening, and we don't have all that long." Jordan left Brady to make the call.

Once he was out of sight, Brady leaned against his desk.

What am I getting myself into?

Chapter Ten

THE sight of the house was enough to send ribbons of panic fluttering through Brady's belly. "Wow. This is beautiful." *And big. Don't forget big.* Brady's entire apartment could probably fit into it at least six times over. The long, imposing path that led to the equally imposing front door made his heart quake. *This is stupid. His mother is going to see right through this whole scheme.*

"Relax," Jordan said quietly. "It's just dinner. She doesn't eat guests." He leaned in closer. "Okay, so she may nibble them around the edges a little."

"Not helping," Brady gritted out. The ride over there had been bad enough. He'd tried his hardest not to think about the approaching inquisition, but his mind had refused to cooperate. Still, it was too late to back out now, not when the door was already opening and—

Jordan reached down and clasped his hand, and warmth surged through him. *That's nice.*

Brady took a deep breath and pasted on a smile.

The woman who opened the door was unquestionably Jordan's sister. They shared the same dark complexion, the same large, dark eyes. Her gaze flickered down to their joined hands.

She blinked and jerked her head up to stare at Brady before straightening and smiling at Jordan. "Hey. You didn't tell us you were bringing a guest."

Jordan grinned. "I wanted it to be a surprise." He stepped past her into the hallway, pulling Brady with him.

"Oh, it's definitely that," she muttered under her breath. Once the door was closed, she turned to Brady. "Hi. I'm Fiona, Jordan's sister."

"Brady Donovan."

Her eyes widened, and she gaped at Jordan. "Your personal assistant? I know I said don't lose him, but *Jesus*, Jordan—dating him? Don't you think that's a little... extreme?"

Jordan smirked. "You know, 'pleased to meet you, Brady' would have been perfectly adequate in the circumstances."

Brady was still a little shell-shocked by her reaction. Fortunately, Fiona appeared to have recovered her manners. She held out her hand. "I'm glad to meet you, Brady. Jordan has spoken very highly of you."

Brady blinked. "He has?"

Fiona smiled. "Well, to be honest, I sort of got the impression he couldn't run that company without you. It must be true, then. Behind every great man is a great...." She bit her lip.

"Man," Jordan suggested with a wicked smile. "And when you've let go of his hand, maybe we should introduce him to Mom?"

Fiona released Brady's hand quickly. "She's in the conservatory. It's orchid-misting time." She led them along the hallway, with Brady trying his best not to be overwhelmed by the sheer size of the place. Warm oak floorboards complemented gleaming white woodwork and pale cream walls, accentuated by watercolors here and there.

The conservatory was a large space with walls of glass that looked out over a stunning garden. Every windowsill contained pots of the most beautiful orchids Brady had ever seen. Large fleshy pink petals, next to more delicate, almost translucent flowers, their dark green leaves glossy and healthy.

Jordan's mother was tall, her silver-gray hair done in an intricate knot at the back. She was talking to a man dressed in a navy suit, who was nodding as she spoke. He glanced up as they approached, and for a moment Brady felt decidedly shabby in comparison, in his black pants, pale blue shirt, dark blue bow tie, and black woolen cardigan. Jordan had assured him that he was perfectly dressed for the occasion, but still….

Jordan's mother frowned, the lines marring her smooth brow, but then she straightened her features. "Jordan? You should have told me you were also bringing a guest." She lowered her gaze to where Jordan took hold of Brady's hand, curling his fingers around it. A slow smile blossomed. She put down her water bottle, walked over to them, and extended a hand to Brady. "Hello. I'm Lynne Wolf, Jordan's mother. And you are…?"

"Brady Donovan, ma'am." He took her cool hand in his, noting that Jordan didn't relinquish his hold. "I work with Jordan."

From behind them, Fiona snickered. "He's the one you should thank for the beautiful flowers for your birthday, Mom."

Jordan growled low. "Thanks, Fi."

She chuckled. "Anytime, bro."

Lynne ignored them both. "Thank you for joining us, Brady. I wish I could say Jordan's spoken of you, but—"

"But seeing as this is a very recent development," Jordan interjected, "that's understandable." Then Brady's heart skipped a beat when Jordan leaned in and kissed him lightly on the cheek. "You're meeting him now, though." Jordan straightened and glanced over at the man in the suit. "You must be Corbin. Hi."

Corbin gave him a quick nod. "Hey." His gaze flicked from Lynne to Fiona, then back to Jordan. "Sorry, dude. This is a little… awkward."

Fiona cleared her throat. "How about I fix us all a cocktail? Dinner won't be for an hour or so. Dad's in his den. I'll go bang on his door."

"Cocktails. Delightful idea. Jordan, why don't you take Corbin and Brady through into the drawing room? I'll be with you when I've finished in here."

Jordan nodded, then led them out of the conservatory.

Brady liked the drawing room instantly. It was a nice size, with three sofas arranged in a U shape around a fireplace. In one corner of the room was a drinks cabinet, and to the left, french windows opened out onto the garden.

Corbin sat on the sofa nearest the drinks cabinet, leaning forward, his elbows on his knees. "Okay, while we have a moment to ourselves…." He gave Jordan an apologetic glance. "Your sister persuaded me to come along, but I had no idea you were already attached. Judging by their reactions, neither did she or your mom. So in the circumstances, maybe I should go?"

Jordan shook his head. "Nonsense. One, you'll miss out on a good dinner, and two, you have no reason whatsoever to feel awkward. No one asked them to do this, okay? If anyone should be feeling awkward, it's them."

Brady had to say something. "Listen, if anyone should leave, it's me. I'm the unexpected guest, after all." When Jordan stared at him, obviously unhappy, Brady gave him a reassuring smile. "Relax. I'm not leaving either." He snickered. "You never mentioned that your sister is a brat." It was a bold move, but hell, he was there as Jordan's boyfriend.

Gotta keep in character, right?

Corbin smothered a snicker. "What gave it away?" He grinned. "I get to say that—I'm her supervisor. And after this, she is going to owe me, big-time." He gave Brady a warm smile. "Again, I'm sorry, man. I didn't mean to tread on anybody's toes. From the look of things, you got the best sibling."

Brady glanced across at Jordan and smiled. "I did, didn't I?" Jordan's brief, startled blink was adorable, but Brady had to remind himself not to bury himself in the part.

Fiona bustled into the room. "This looks cozy. What would you all like to drink?"

"She makes a mean margarita," Jordan said with a smile. Brady liked that he was being pleasant to his sister, brat or not. Then Jordan's eyes gleamed with mischief. "So… you brought your boss, huh?"

Fiona glared at Corbin. "Thanks for that."

Corbin gazed back at her, keeping his face straight.

Brady had a feeling Jordan was correct—it was going to be a very entertaining evening.

"DINNER was great." Jordan relaxed against the seat cushions with Brady next to him.

"I'm sorry about the barbecue idea." Dad peered toward the french windows. "Your mother is right, however. I think we're in for a downpour."

"Are you sure you don't want to stay the night? We have room for all of you."

"Thanks, Mom, but that won't be necessary." Jordan didn't want to put Brady in an awkward situation. He'd been wonderful so far, playing the part to perfection.

After dinner, Fiona had taken Jordan aside and apologized for the scheme. Then she'd chastised him for not telling them all about Brady.

"He's awesome," she exclaimed. "He's funny, intelligent, and he obviously adores you. And if I'd known about him, I wouldn't have twisted Corbin's arm into coming here tonight."

Jordan had his own theory about that. He'd caught several glances in Fiona's direction when Corbin clearly thought no one was looking. "Are you sure he's gay?"

Fiona stilled for a moment. "As a matter of fact, he's not—he's bi. The only other gay guy in the office is married. Corbin was sort of a last-minute idea."

"Mmm-hmm."

Fiona stared at him. "What?"

Jordan smiled. "Nothing."

Brady tugged on his arm, pulling him back into the present. "Earth to Jordan. Your dad just asked if you wanted more coffee."

Jordan shook his head. "I'm fine." He watched as Brady chatted with his parents, relaxed and content. Fiona's words still rang in his head, however.

He obviously adores you.

If Jordan hadn't known better, he'd have said her assumption was correct. Brady looked for all the world like he belonged at Jordan's side. He'd known a ton of guys who'd been less attentive in the short span of their relationships than Brady had been all evening.

A rumble of thunder broke the peaceful setting, and when lightning jagged across the sky, illuminating the trees, his mom shivered. "Jordan, you can't travel in this weather. Please, reconsider. I've already made up the bed in the room that used to be yours."

Brady gave him a startled glance, and Jordan knew exactly what had just gone through his mind. "Er, Mom, that's really kind of you, but...." Brady hadn't signed up to share a bed for the night, and there was no way Jordan was about to put him on the spot.

Thankfully his mother was quick on the uptake. "Brady can have the room next to yours, if that's okay."

There was no mistaking the relief in Brady's expression, and for one illogical moment, Jordan was dismayed. *Well, I guess that makes it obvious how he really feels about me, if the prospect of sleeping in the same bed is so abhorrent.* He had no clue why such a thought would send waves of disappointment through him.

"Is that all right with you?" Jordan asked.

Brady nodded. "I think she has a point. It's getting really bad out there." Right on cue, another rumble of thunder, this one much louder, rattled the windows, and he shivered, his eyes wide, edging closer to Jordan.

It took a moment for his actions to sink in. Brady—his wonderful, fearless assistant, capable and organized—was afraid of thunder and lightning.

Jordan reached for his hand and squeezed it. "We're safe in here. And somehow I don't think the house is about to get struck by lightning."

Brady gave him a grateful smile. "Good to know."

"Corbin, you'll stay, won't you?" his mom asked.

Corbin nodded, his eyes meeting Fiona's for the briefest moment. Jordan chuckled to himself when the merest hint of a blush stole over her cheeks. *Aha.* Fi wasn't as oblivious as he'd supposed.

The rest of the evening was a pleasant surprise. Dad got out board games that Jordan hadn't seen for years: Clue, Headache, Trouble…. Jordan couldn't remember the last time he'd had such a fun time. He, Brady, Fiona, and Corbin sat around the square coffee table, playing Clue, while their parents watched, Mom working on her cross-stitch and Dad reading. Outside, the storm worsened, and it was noticeable how Brady didn't move from Jordan's side. When the lights flickered and Dad made noises about going to check the generator, Brady held on tight to Jordan's hand.

"I know it's illogical," Brady said quietly, "but I've always hated thunder and lightning, ever since I was a kid. Mom says I used to hide under my bed, clutching a blanket."

Right then the power died, and gasps rang out from everyone.

"Don't worry, the backup generator will kick in soon." Mom sounded her usual calm self. "In the meantime, Fiona and I will go into the kitchen and find the candles, in case this continues. Jordan, you stay here with Brady. Corbin, could you go down to the basement and see if my husband needs any help getting the generator going? It can be a little temperamental."

"Sure."

When it was just him and Brady left alone in the drawing room, Jordan took his hand. "You doing okay?"

To his surprise Brady rested his head on Jordan's shoulder. "I'll be fine." The ominous roll of a thunderclap pulled a gasp from him, and he shivered again.

Jordan couldn't help his response. He put his arm around Brady and held him close. "It's all right. I've got you. You're safe." Brady turned his face up toward him, and for one brief, illogical moment, Jordan was overwhelmed by the urge to kiss that soft-looking mouth. Brady seemed to be holding his breath, his eyes locked on Jordan's, the round disks of his glasses reflecting the lightning that lit up the sky beyond the window.

"Jordan," he whispered.

"There, that's better." Mom came into the room, carrying a candelabra loaded with three candles. Fiona followed her with another.

Brady jumped as if burned and pulled away, and Jordan was once more beset with disappointment. Holding Brady had felt... good, but there was suddenly distance between them, and Jordan regretted the loss of intimacy.

The lights came on, and Mom beamed. "I knew they could get that old beast to work. *Now* perhaps he'll listen to me when I say it's time to get a new one."

Brady wasn't meeting Jordan's gaze.

"Oh, I don't know." Fiona's eyes twinkled. "I think there's something to be said for candlelight. Very romantic, don't you think, Jordan?" Her gaze flickered toward Brady.

"This calls for hot chocolate," Mom said decisively. "Nothing like it when there's a storm raging. Don't you agree, Brady?"

He smiled. "Hot chocolate is always good, in my opinion."

Jordan didn't want to talk about hot chocolate. He wanted Brady back in his arms, just the two of them.

What the hell just happened?

BRADY stiffened as the bedroom door opened and Jordan entered. He was still ashamed of his behavior earlier, acting like some scared little wussy kid. *What must he think of me?* Brady couldn't get over how it had felt to be held like he was something precious, and all he'd wanted was Jordan's lips on his, to lose himself in the kiss he'd dreamed about for so long.

He still couldn't decide whether Lynne's entrance at that moment had been good timing, or the worst ever.

I wanted him. And what if I had kissed him? What then?

Such actions would have consequences.

"Do you have everything you need?" Jordan asked. "There are more blankets in the closet if you get cold in the night. And I'll be right next door."

"Does that mean I can climb into your bed and hide from the storm?" Brady kept his tone lighthearted. When Jordan blinked, he chuckled. "Yeah, like I'd do that." Except he would, in a heartbeat. "Listen, I didn't think you'd be okay with us sharing a bed, not under your parents' roof and all."

Jordan nodded. "My mom may act like she's this liberal-minded, twenty-first century mother, but when it comes down to her son sleeping with this guy she's only just heard about? I think even she might balk at that."

Much as Brady really, *really* liked the idea of spending the night in Jordan's bed, what scared him to his core was that Jordan might see too much. That he'd somehow see right through Brady's act, see the desire that lay deep inside him.

Rain lashed against the window, but the thunder had passed, thankfully. Brady smiled. "I don't think there'll be any need for me to be knocking on your door. Your mom gave me a new toothbrush. I've got everything I need."

But not what he really wanted.

"I'll say good night, then." Yet Jordan didn't move.

You need to go, Brady told him silently. *Before I do something I might regret.*

Like kiss him. Hold him. Undress him.

"Good night," he said softly, not moving from beside the bed.

Finally Jordan nodded, turned around, and left the room, closing the door quietly behind him.

Brady sank onto the mattress and put his head in his hands. His heart had never been so conflicted. And he was going to put it through the emotional wringer all over again the following weekend.

Why did I say yes to this? I must be crazy.

He hadn't given a moment's thought to what life would be like after the party was over. Would things go back to the way they had been?

Brady had no clue.

He climbed into the bed, switched off the lamp beside it, pulled the covers over his head, and hid himself from the world.

Chapter Eleven

BRADY watched the car until it had turned the corner, then slowly climbed the steps to the front door. He felt kind of... deflated. Jordan had been quiet for the trip home, apart from thanking him for the visit and apologizing that they'd had to spend the night there. Then he was gone.

Brady glanced up at the sky above. It was hard to believe the previous night had been so turbulent; not a cloud was in sight, as if the storm had washed them all away.

Once inside the building, he trudged up the stairs to the second floor, just as Phil was coming down from the third.

"Hey. It's a real mess up there." She pointed toward the roof.

"Why? What's happened?"

Phil widened her eyes. "Didn't you hear it last night?"

Brady sighed. "What have I missed? I was in Westchester last night."

"Then you missed all the drama. We've lost the birch. Lightning struck it." Her face fell. "And it was growing into such a nice shape too." Phil cocked her head to one side. "Was that your boss who just dropped you off? I was at my window when your car pulled up."

"Yeah, that was him." Brady's stomach clenched.

Phil studied him closely. "Hey, are you okay?"

It was on the tip of his tongue to say everything was fine, but he stopped himself. Maybe talking about it would clear his thoughts. "You got time for a coffee?"

Phil smiled. "I was just on my way to mail a letter, but that can wait. It won't get collected until tomorrow anyway. Why don't you come on up to my place? There's more than half a pot already brewed."

"That sounds good. Let me get rid of my jacket and change into clean clothes. I was wearing these yesterday." He shrugged. "I didn't exactly plan on spending the night away."

Phil chuckled. "Westchester is beginning to sound intriguing. Come up when you're ready." She turned around and headed back upstairs.

Brady let himself into his apartment, shucked off his jacket, and hurried into his bedroom. He deposited his clothes in the hamper, then pulled on jeans and a sweater. When he got to Phil's door, it was ajar, but he knocked before entering.

"Come on in."

Phil's apartment was painted in a warm sunny yellow, and she had a seat below the two windows that looked out onto the street. The first thing Brady noticed was a tabby cat, its eyes closed and paws tucked under its chest.

"I didn't know you had a kitty."

Phil laughed. "Hardly surprising. He doesn't leave the apartment. Toeby is definitely not a street kitty. And that's Toeby spelled T-O-E-B-Y, on account of his extra toes."

"Wow." Brady went over to the cushioned seat and sat next to the cat, who blinked and stretched before immediately climbing into his lap. "Well, hello there, Mr. Polydactyl Kitty."

Toeby put his paws on Brady's chest and rubbed his head under Brady's chin.

Phil snorted. "Toeby, you are such an attention whore. You'll take cuddles from anyone." She grinned at Brady. "You didn't intend on moving from that spot for the next three hours, right?" Phil handed him a mug, then sat beside him. Brady stroked Toeby, who had once again curled up into a ball, only this time in his lap. "So, who lives in Westchester?"

Brady took a sip of coffee before replying. "My boss's parents."

Phil stared at him. "Your *boss* took you to meet his *parents*? What the hell? Are you dating your boss, or something?"

"I wish." When Phil stayed silent, Brady glanced across at her. She was still staring at him. Brady sighed. "It's a long story."

Phil leaned against the window. "We've got time. Besides, you're not going anywhere for a while, not if Toeby has anything to do with it."

She had a point. And sitting drinking coffee, stroking a warm, purring kitty, wasn't exactly an unpleasant situation to be in. He took another drink, then started his tale at the point where Jordan had first visited the apartment. Phil listened intently, occasionally reaching across to scratch Toeby behind the ears or under his chin.

When Brady finished, Phil expelled a long breath. "Wow. And here was I, thinking the life of a personal assistant wasn't all that exciting." She peered closely at him. "When did you first know?"

Brady frowned. "Know what?"

"That you were in love with Jordan."

"Whoa. Wait a minute. When did I say that?" Brady gaped at her. "I never said that."

She huffed. "You didn't have to. It's written all over you." She smiled. "Now, if it had been *me* in a blackout with a guy I had the hots for, I would have totally taken the opportunity to sneak in a kiss."

"With his parents and sister—not to mention his sister's boss—about to walk back into the room at any second? Yeah, right."

Phil grinned. "What about later? You know, when the thunder roared and the lightning flashed? That would have been the perfect excuse to tap on his bedroom door." She shrugged. "Still, all is not lost. You have next weekend, right? You can put the moves on him then."

"Who says I'm *going* to put any moves on him?" Brady couldn't believe what she was saying.

Phil sighed. "So you're just gonna go there, act like you're his BF, then it's back to work the Monday after like nothing happened?"

Brady struggled to find the words to make her see the reality of the situation. "Okay, here's the thing. One, I'm not in love with him. It's just… a crush, all right? And two, he's my boss," he said gently. "I can't make a move on my boss."

"Why not? Bosses have affairs with their secretaries all the time."

"But I'm not his secretary. And who says I want an affair?" What he really wanted was something longer-lasting than a roll between the sheets and being taken out to dinner now and then. Brady didn't want Mr. Right Now—he wanted Mr. Right.

Phil pursed her lips. "Well, you obviously want *something* to happen between you. Suppose you do let him know how you feel. What if he feels the same way about you?"

Brady wanted to tell her that the universe didn't work like that. "And what if he doesn't? Suddenly I'm out of a job."

"Then let's talk about this job of yours." Phil put down her mug and folded her arms across her chest. "Do you want to stay in a job where you have an unrequited crush on your boss? What if... what if he meets someone? How are you gonna feel then?"

Brady did *not* want to contemplate that situation, but Phil wasn't done.

"Let's go one stage further. How are you gonna feel when he's asking *you* to make dinner reservations for him and Mr. BF? Hotel reservations? Hmm? How are you gonna feel, when you *know* he's shacked up in some hotel, screwing his boyfriend, and all because *you* didn't have the balls to come out and say, 'Hey, guess what? I really like you'?"

Something deep in Brady's belly rolled over, sending a wave of nausea through him.

"So the way I see it, you have three options. One, you say nothing, just continue the way things are, and hope to God you don't end up organizing your boss's love life. Two, you decide that you're willing to give up your job, because Option One sounds like torture, and you find another. Which wouldn't be a problem for you. Or... there's Option Three."

"Which is what?"

Phil gave him a gentle smile. "You take a chance and tell him how you feel." She leaned forward and patted his knee. "And while we're on the subject? This sounds like *way* more than a crush. Maybe you need to think about how badly you want this guy in your life. Because from where I'm sitting?" Her eyes shone. "Sure sounds like love to me."

Toeby chose that moment to butt his head under Brady's chin.

"See? Toebs agrees with me."

Brady let out a soft sigh. "You make it sound so... easy."

"I'm sure it isn't, but when I saw you on the stairs just now, you seemed so miserable, and that's not right." She paused for a moment. "Visiting you when you were sick, buying you clothes, taking you to dinner.... Those don't sound like the actions of someone who doesn't care about you. Maybe there *is* something there. But you'll never know until you take a chance. And next weekend sounds like the perfect opportunity." She cocked her head again. "How did it feel, pretending to be his boyfriend? Did you get along with his family?"

Brady had to admit, Jordan's family was amazing. They'd treated him warmly and made him feel comfortable and welcome. That morning when the time came to leave, Lynne had taken him aside and said she hoped to see him again. Jordan's dad had shaken his hand and said what a great time they'd had the previous evening. And Fiona had given him a hug, which really took him by surprise.

"I liked them." As for the playacting, it had been difficult to remember that it *was* an act, that they weren't really a couple. Especially when Jordan had held him in the dark, so close that his breath stirred Brady's hair, his lips scant inches away from Brady's....

Phil was right. He couldn't go on like this. And waiting to see if Jordan felt the same might take... forever.

No, if anyone was going to make the first move, it would have to be Brady.

He scritched Toeby's ears, and the kitty's motorboat of a purr vibrated through his lap.

"Cats are great when it comes to decision-making," Phil said with a smile. "They sit there, they listen, they take it all in, and they never judge, as long as you're giving them enough love."

"And what makes you think I've come to a decision?" Brady asked her.

Phil's smile widened. "Have you *any* idea how easy you are to read?" Her eyes sparkled. "Is Jordan always focused on his work?"

"Pretty much."

She nodded slowly. "That explains it. He can't see what's right in front of him. *But*, get him relaxed and that might change." Phil chuckled. "Damn, I'd love to be a fly on the wall next weekend."

Brady didn't want to think about that, not when they had a whole week of work ahead of them. Then he remembered. "Aw, hell."

"What's wrong?"

"Jordan's booked us into his favorite spa on Thursday afternoon. Haircut, manicure... massage...."

Phil giggled. "Ooh, I like it. Bare flesh, sauna, everything getting... steamy."

Brady glared at her. "That is *not* helpful." Not for the first time, the thought of a butt-naked Jordan, his skin glistening with sweat, filtered through Brady's head, and he squirmed on his seat.

Phil snorted. "I was trying to show you how far gone you are on him. Seeing your... reaction?" She smirked. "My work here is done." She got up and went toward the kitchen area.

Brady wanted to say something, to protest—anything. Instead, he resorted to the only defense he had left. "You're a bitch, you know that?"

Her laugh told him, yeah, she knew. And Toeby's wiseass yawn merely confirmed it.

Chapter Twelve

JORDAN had no clue why he was nervous, but as he pushed open the main door to the office, his belly did a little flip-flop at the sight of Brady, standing there with his newspapers.

"Good morning." Jordan affected a calm he certainly didn't feel.

Brady gave his usual smile. "Good morning. Your coffee is on, and your mail is on your desk." He handed Jordan the papers.

They walked in silence, side by side, along the hallway to Brady's office. Once inside, Jordan's nostrils were assailed by the aroma of the freshly brewed coffee. "When you bring in the tray, bring a cup for yourself too."

"Oh. Certainly, sir."

That last word brought home to Jordan what was wrong with the situation. Hearing "sir" on Brady's lips, after the shopping trip and the visit to his parents' house, felt all kinds of wrong.

He walked into his office, deposited the papers on his desk, then hung up his jacket, his stomach still churning. He'd set events in motion that had irrevocably changed their office dynamic, and it was up to him to find a modus operandi that felt more... normal. Because he couldn't continue like this.

When Brady entered with the tray, Jordan sat on the couch. "You can pour, then join me here please."

Brady nodded. He placed the two large cups on the table in front of them, then sat at Jordan's side. Neither of them spoke for a moment, and the silence only added to the knot in Jordan's belly.

"Brady," he began, his voice low. "Don't you think addressing me as 'sir' sounds a little... odd, considering the situation?"

Brady blinked. "The *situation* is that we're in the office. Surely that's how I should address you?"

"And that doesn't feel weird? After Friday? Saturday?" Jordan sighed. "Of all the staff in this office, you are the one who works most closely with me." He gestured to the door. "Everyone out there... *they* get to call me sir, but not you. Not now." He peered closely at Brady. "Can you live with that?"

Brady picked up his cup and took a sip from it. Finally, he nodded. "Sure. You're right, of course. I didn't want to overstep any boundaries. That's all."

Jordan smiled, the tension inside him easing a little. "Considering how much of my life you get to see, I think losing the 'sir' part is way overdue." He leaned back. "And now that we've got *that* settled, let's go through my schedule, okay?"

Brady drew in a deep breath. When his smile reached his eyes, Jordan was flooded with a sense of relief.

"Sure… Jordan." Brady chuckled. "Still sounds a bit strange, but I guess I'll get used to it." He got up from the couch. "I'll go get my tablet."

Jordan waited until Brady had left the room before expelling a long breath.

We're not out of the woods yet.

It wasn't just the way Brady addressed him. It was the way Jordan felt when Brady was near him, like he was suddenly more aware of him than ever before.

And Jordan had no idea what to do about the way he was feeling.

BRADY got out of the car and glanced up at the shiny black-granite-and-glass storefront, bearing only three words: Spiff for Men. It certainly seemed like a large place.

"It's funny. The number of times I've booked you in here, and I had no clue what the place was like."

"It's the kind of place where they have boxes of cigars if their clients want to smoke with their coffee," Jordan said, joining him. "There's a roof terrace."

Brady shivered. "Not today, I think. It's too cold." He peered at Jordan. "You know I've never done anything like this, right?" He wasn't too sure what to expect.

Jordan laughed. "Relax. This is my treat. We'll start with a massage, steaming hot towels, a facial, and then we'll have a haircut, pedicure, and manicure. Plus a really good, close shave."

Brady smiled and stroked his chin. "Do I need that?"

To his surprise Jordan reached across and rubbed a thumb along his jawline. It was an intimate moment, and Brady had to struggle to repress his shiver of desire. *God, what he does to me....*

"Trust me. A hot towel to relax, followed by an old-fashioned straight razor shave? You'll feel amazing after." Jordan put his hand to Brady's back and guided him through the glass door. Once they'd checked in at the reception desk, a young woman led them along a hallway to a darkened room with an adjoining door. A massage table sat in the center of the room, and next to it was a stand where bottles of oil sat, along with candles flickering in glasses. Brady detected the faint aroma of lavender and something else.

"Gentlemen, you can get undressed through there in the changing room," she told them. "There are towels for you. Shawn will be in here, and Dominic will be in the other massage room. When they're done, Shena and I will come in to do your facials." She left them.

Brady shook his head. "I'm feeling really pampered right now, and they haven't even started yet."

Jordan chuckled. "Wait until Dominic is kneading your back like it's a piece of dough." When Brady stared at him, Jordan laughed. "Okay, I'm lying. It's nothing like that. The massage is more like a full-body exfoliating treatment. I just made it sound like a visit to a chiropractor."

Brady rolled his eyes. "And I believed you." He followed Jordan into the changing room, where a rail with hangers stood against one wall, and on a cabinet sat a pile of folded white towels. He hesitated for a moment, glancing around the small, neat space.

Jordan stood very still. "Shy? Just pretend it's the locker room back in high school."

Brady snorted. "That actually doesn't help. I spent most of *my* time in the locker room trying to peek at Chase Garton without him realizing I was doing it."

"Chase Garton?"

Brady sighed. "My first crush." It didn't help matters that he was having this conversation with his current crush, except part of him knew Phil was right—he'd passed crush a while back.

"Did anything every happen between you?" Jordan asked as he took off his jacket, loosened and removed his tie, then unbuttoned his shirt. Trying his best not to stare, Brady busied himself with the removal of his bow tie, but his fingers and thumbs had other ideas. He envied Jordan his calm, unruffled state.

"Unfortunately not. Chase only had eyes for Amanda Pettifer at the time. I doubt I even registered on his radar."

"Nothing so sad as unrequited love." Jordan slipped off his shoes, socks, and pants, pausing when all that remained were his black briefs.

Brady chose that moment to gaze at a print on the wall while he finished undressing. He was *not* about to turn around, not while there was the remotest possibility of coming face-to-face with Jordan's dick. Keeping his back to Jordan, he quickly removed his boxers and grabbed one of the towels—and froze as his fingers met Jordan's.

"Here, you take that one." Jordan handed him the top towel.

Brady couldn't help himself. He took the towel, his gaze drifting down Jordan's firm torso, noting the hair that covered his chest, growing sparser as it reached his navel, forming a dark trail that led down to his dick—his half-hard dick, springing from a nest of tight curls, his body hair covering his thighs in a soft-looking down.

A fully clothed Jordan was a sight to behold. Naked Jordan was just... beautiful.

Brady averted his gaze, unfolded the wide towel, and wrapped it around himself. "Ready." He was dismayed that the word popped out as a croak.

The gleam in Jordan's eyes could have been amusement. "You get Dominic, so you're through there," he said, pointing to another door. "I'll see you later."

Brady walked out of the changing room, to where a man dressed in black pants and a tee awaited him. He gestured to the table. "Good afternoon. Hop up onto the table under your towel please." He gave Brady a polite smile. "Have you ever had a massage before?"

Brady shook his head. "Although I've heard Jordan speak enough times about Shawn's technique." He removed his towel and climbed onto the table, facedown, arranging the towel to cover his butt.

Dominic snickered. "Yeah, Jordan likes to really feel it. I won't be giving you the same treatment, unless you specifically ask for it." He stepped closer, holding a bowl containing what looked like wipes. "I'm going to cleanse the skin first, then apply the exfoliating scrub all over. I'll massage it into the skin, and it'll feel a little gritty. Once that's done, I'll remove all traces of it, and then I'll do a full-body massage. I don't usually use the scrub on the chest area, but I will have you roll over and continue the massage. By the end of it, you should feel relaxed and soothed. Have you had an exfoliating treatment before?"

Brady smiled. "We're talking total newbie here."

Dominic grinned. "You'll love it."

Brady pressed his face into the padded hole, and seconds later, Dominic wiped over his back. The scrub was indeed gritty, and Dominic rubbed over the skin in slow circles. It was strangely soothing, and Brady lost himself in the sensations. The air was filled with a pleasant perfume, and soft music played in the background. All in all, it was a very sensual experience, and Brady could understand why Jordan liked it.

Brady caught a low groan from the other room, and Dominic snickered. "Looks like Shawn found a knot."

Brady was about to speak when Dominic removed the towel and began massaging his ass with firm strokes. Brady let out a tiny squeak, but Dominic had already moved on, stroking down the back of his thighs with strong, capable fingers. When it was time to remove the last traces of the scrub, Brady was well and truly at ease, his body limp beneath Dominic's experienced hands.

The massage was amazing. Subtle aromas reached his nostrils as Dominic manipulated his back muscles. Brady winced slightly when Dominic kneaded his shoulders.

"That's where your tension collects," Dominic told him. "Here and in your neck muscles. Shena gives a fantastic head and neck massage that will really help. You could do with a regular shoulder rub to keep loosened up."

The only problem Brady could see with *that* idea was that there was no one to administer it. He smiled to himself. "Hey, Jordan, here's an idea," he shouted out. "We turn one of the offices into a massage therapy room, and you employ a masseur on a permanent basis. The staff would love it."

Jordan's snort was audible. "Mm-hmm. And they'd spend more time in the therapy room than at their desks," he hollered back.

He had a point. Brady could already see himself booking another appointment. Not often, but now and again, when he needed to de-stress.

"Okay, roll over onto your back."

Brady did as instructed. He closed his eyes, trying not to imagine how Jordan looked right then, his body glistening with oil while Shawn's hands moved over Jordan's chest and belly. He tried not to imagine Jordan's butt, firm and round, covered with the same soft-looking down as his thighs.

Why do I have to have such a good imagination?

A cough brought him sharply into the moment. Dominic was gazing at him, his eyebrows arched slightly, his lips twitching. "Well? Was I right?"

Brady smiled. "Yeah, you were right. I love this." He was grateful Dominic had replaced his towel. Whether his dick was reacting to his imagination or to Dominic's sensual massage, Brady wasn't entirely certain, but he was glad Jordan couldn't see the result.

"You've gone quiet," Jordan called out. He sounded totally relaxed.

Brady chuckled. "Shh. I'm enjoying this."

"I'm glad." There was a pause. "Maybe we should make this a regular thing. You need to take time to relax too. You work very hard."

Above him, Dominic chuckled. "Look who's talking," he murmured.

Brady liked that. Then he remembered Jordan had been speaking to him. "I like the way you look after your staff," he called out with a sigh.

Jordan chuckled. "You're the only one I'm bringing here."

Brady liked that even more.

BRADY stared at his reflection. His hair, usually long on top and swept back, had been shortened, and Matt had shaved the sides and back. It wasn't that drastic a change, and yet Brady hardly recognized himself. It was a sleek, fashionable Brady who stared back at him, with the smoothest jaw Brady had ever experienced. Shena was finishing his manicure, while Debra massaged his other hand.

"So which was your favorite part?" Jordan sat in the chair next to his, while Matt snipped at his hair. Jordan chuckled. "I still think you should have gone for the fish."

Brady shuddered. Even the idea of having fish nibbling at his feet sent shivers through him. "Thank you, but no. I'll stick with the old-fashioned way." He'd enjoyed sitting there with his feet immersed in bubbling warm water, with a glass of champagne on the wide arm of the chair. A thought struck him. "Wait a minute. I didn't see a fish pedicure on the menu. I only found out they do that here because you told me they—" He glared at Jordan. "You made that up, didn't you?"

Jordan chuckled again. "It was certainly entertaining, watching your reaction. Nearly as entertaining as the foot rub. You nearly hit the ceiling when she tried to massage your arches."

"I can't help it if I'm ticklish," Brady remonstrated. He had to admit, however, that he was incredibly relaxed. "I think the massage was the best part." Then he recalled his reaction. "Although you might have warned me. I had no idea he was going to massage my butt."

Jordan coughed. "Ah. Well. They do that when you remove your underwear. They assume you're okay with it."

Brady opened his eyes wide. "And you didn't think to mention this while we were undressing?"

Jordan smirked. "Of course not. It was more entertaining that way."

Brady rolled his eyes.

"I was serious, by the way," Jordan said. "I know I come here once a month—you should join me. No work talk, just the pair of us being pampered, pummeled, and primped."

Brady really liked that idea. "I've checked the weather report for the weekend. No rain forecast, but it'll be cold."

Jordan smiled. "I'll bet you've already emailed Donna to make sure she packs sweaters."

Brady laughed. "This morning." His heartbeat sped up at the thought of spending a whole weekend in Jordan's company. He hadn't packed yet—that was his task when he got home.

"Brady… thanks again."

Brady frowned. "For what?"

"Agreeing to do this. You didn't have to say yes, just because I'm your boss."

He smiled. "If I didn't want to go, I'd have said so. I'm looking forward to it, to be honest." Except what came to mind was Phil's suggestion. Brady still didn't know if he'd have the nerve to say anything, should the occasion arise.

Let's just play this by ear.

Chapter Thirteen

JORDAN was about to message Brady to tell him the car was parked outside his building when the front door opened and he appeared. Jordan caught his breath at the sight. Brady wore the leather biker jacket and black jeans, but what struck Jordan immediately was the absence of glasses.

He looked… amazing.

Brady approached the car, carrying a small suitcase and suit bag. He smiled as Jordan opened the rear car door. "Right on time." The driver got out to take his bags, and Brady climbed into the back beside Jordan. "So… do I pass?"

Jordan swallowed, his throat suddenly dry. Brady was an attractive guy, but the total effect gave him a whole new look. Jordan cocked his head to one side. "Contacts?"

Brady nodded. "I figured it was about time I wore them. I mean, what's the point of buying them if I don't get any use out of them?" He blinked a couple of times. "I've had these in for about two hours, and so far, so good. I don't suppose I look all that different without the glasses."

Jordan would have to disagree. Brady looked gorgeous.

He cleared his throat. "You definitely pass," he said at last. "I like the look. Not that I dislike the glasses, you understand, but this is… different."

Brady's shy smile lit up his eyes. "Thank you. I didn't want to let you down."

Jordan sighed. "Like I said before—there's no way you could ever do that. Just… be yourself."

The driver got back into the car, and they pulled away from the curb.

Brady shook his head. "Is it weird that I feel like I'm playing hooky? I swear, you're a bad influence. Shopping trips, spa afternoons, now this party…." He grinned. "No one would think you had a business to run."

"Speaking of which…." Jordan gave him a hard stare. "No work talk this weekend. We're going to relax and enjoy ourselves. And that's an order."

Brady gave a mini salute. "Yes, sir. And before you ask, that's the last time I'll say the word." He leaned back, his head supported by the leather rest as he gazed out at the passing scenery.

Jordan had to fight hard not to stare. *I seem to be doing that a lot lately.* He'd certainly struggled to keep his gaze off Brady while they'd changed out of their clothes. With each passing day, he saw more and more of the man who'd remained hidden from his sight for so long.

How did I miss him?

Jordan had no clue, but the idea of spending more time getting to know Brady was very pleasant indeed.

JORDAN chuckled. "Huckleberry Lane. It conjures up an image of quaint houses, don't you think?"

Brady stared out of the car window. "I don't think any of these could be described as 'quaint.'"

Jordan had to agree. So far, the estate seemed to comprise very large, free-standing townhouses with huge front lawns and long, snaking driveways. Drake's house was no different. Its pale blue clapboard exterior and vaulted roof gave it an imposing air. Already, four or five cars filled the gravel drive, spreading out along the lane.

Jordan found a space and parked. He switched off the engine and peered through the windshield at the house. "It *is* beautiful." He liked the triangular window that followed the line of the roof.

They got out of the car and walked around to the trunk to collect their bags. Brady glanced toward the house. "It looks like quite a few guests are already here."

"I know I should have asked before, but what did you send Drake and Belinda as their anniversary gift?"

Brady smiled as they approached the house. "*You* sent a flower arrangement and a bottle of vintage champagne—2002, bottled the same year they got married."

Jordan shook his head. "You're amazing. What would I do without you?" *And I hope I never have to find out.* It was a situation he did *not* want to contemplate.

"It seemed an appropriate gift," Brady said with a shrug.

On impulse, Jordan seized his hand and squeezed it. "It was perfect." He didn't want to relinquish his hold of Brady's hand, and Brady didn't try to pull free of his grasp. "And before we get in there, can I just say...." Jordan was suddenly lost for words. He desperately wanted to convey his gratitude, his reassurance that it was going to be okay, that Brady would make him proud if he were standing there in his usual office attire, but his throat tightened at the sight of Brady's earnest expression.

His heartbeat stuttered when Brady leaned forward and kissed his cheek. "Jordan? Ring the bell?" It was as if Brady, too, was struggling to find the words. The simple yet intimate gesture said enough.

Before Jordan could raise his hand to the bell, the front door opened and Belinda stood there in a dark blue dress, with a simple string of pearls around her neck. "Jordan. It's been far too long." When they stepped inside and she closed the door, Belinda seized Jordan in a warm hug. "It's good to see you." She released him and turned to Brady, her hand outstretched. "Hi, I'm Belinda Daniels. I'm so glad you could join us this weekend."

"Brady Donovan. And thank you for having me."

Belinda smiled. "Any friend of Jordan's is welcome here." She returned her attention to Jordan. "Thank you for the beautiful flowers, by the way. And that champagne was inspired!"

Jordan smiled. "I'm glad you liked them. Happy anniversary."

Belinda beamed. "I have *so* been looking forward to this weekend. I was delighted when Drake told me you could make it." She glanced in Brady's direction. "I'm even happier that you brought a guest. Here, give me your jackets. Then I'll show you to your room."

Jordan gazed at the hallway, with its high, sloping ceiling, sunlight pouring in through the skylight above their heads. "Belinda, this is beautiful." Two antique dressers stood against one wall, and a low, long bookcase stood against the other. Above it were three watercolor paintings depicting various coastal scenes. The hallway opened out into another room, also light and airy, from which came the chatter of voices and the sound of music.

Belinda's face glowed. "We like it. The kids love the backyard and the pool, that's for sure. They can't wait to see you, by the way. Marty has been talking about you for days." She led them through a door to the right. "This will be your room. Why don't you freshen up, then join us in the living room? Drake is making cocktails."

It was only once the door closed behind her that the situation hit home.

They were sharing a room.

Evidently the same thought had occurred to Brady. "Did you know we were going to share a room?"

Jordan groaned. "I didn't think. When we spoke on the phone, Drake said something about Belinda wanting to make sure there was a room for me. I completely forgot about it until now."

Brady sighed. "And I didn't ask, because I had nothing to do with the arrangements for this part of the weekend. I just assumed…." He gazed at the oak-framed bed, covered in a blue-and-white comforter. "It's a queen too." The room contained an oak cabinet, a tall, slim bookcase, and a comfortable-looking couch. "I can always sleep on the couch."

Like Jordan would stand for that. "Uh-uh. *I* sleep on the couch. *You* get the bed." When Brady stuck out his chin, Jordan held up his hand. "You're doing me the favor, remember, by coming here. No way will I let you sleep on the couch." It was the only solution. The last thing Jordan wanted was to make Brady uncomfortable, and them sleeping in the same bed seemed above and beyond.

"Are you sure?"

Jordan smiled. "Absolutely. And it's only for two nights, right?"

Brady tilted his head to one side. "Do you usually share a bed with, what's his name... Clive, when you go to weekend functions?"

"If there's only one bed, sure."

"Then—"

Jordan narrowed his gaze. "Brady," he said a low voice.

Brady bit his lip. "Gee, honey, I think we're having our first argument." His eyes twinkled.

It was just the right thing to say. Jordan burst out laughing. "Ready to go mingle with the rest of the guests?"

Brady grinned. "Once I've slipped into character."

Jordan snickered. "Judging by that last remark, I thought you already were." He matched Brady's grin. "Will I be able to tell when you're in character?"

"Sure. I'll be the one gazing at you adoringly whenever some female starts taking too much interest in that shapely ass of yours."

Jordan burst into laughter. "Excuse me? Shapely ass?" He was definitely warming to this new Brady.

Good humor sparkled in Brady's eyes. "See, I can say that now. I've seen it." He arched his eyebrows. "And if you're not happy with the idea of a sassy boyfriend, you'd better tell me now before we get out there and mingle. I can always change the script if you'd prefer a quieter, more deferential version."

Jordan held up his hands defensively. "Far be it from me to argue with your interpretation of the role. I happen to like sassy boyfriends." He nodded toward the door to the bathroom. "Do you want to freshen up?"

Brady glanced down at his slim-fitting white shirt, open at the collar. "Will this do? Or should I change?"

Jordan thought he looked just perfect. "You're fine. Let's go meet the other guests." It occurred to him that he had no idea how many people were going to be there that weekend.

"I'll be right behind you," Brady said with a smile.

That was when it hit Jordan. For all his new confidence, Brady was nervous.

"And I'll be right here," Jordan replied reassuringly. He didn't miss the expression of relief on Brady's face, and his initial reaction was to pull Brady into a hug, to hold him close and let him know it would all be fine. The last thing he wanted was for Brady to feel ill at ease.

The progression had been so gradual that Jordan had hardly noticed, but somehow during the last month, Brady had gone from being an efficient but forgettable PA to a warm, intelligent, funny guy who stirred something deep inside him.

A guy Jordan wanted to spend more time with. His only regret was that Brady was there as a favor to Jordan. This wasn't real, as much as Jordan wanted it to be.

THERE were maybe seven or eight people in the living room, a fairly even mix of men and women. Drake was chatting with his guests as he mixed cocktails in a shaker and poured wine, and a boy and girl—both in their teens, by the look of it—were circulating, handing out canapés. Brady loved how the boy's eyes lit up with genuine delight when he saw Jordan. Brady left Jordan talking eagerly with the kids and went to fetch him a drink.

Drake frowned. "Have we met? I have the strangest feeling I've seen you before."

Brady smiled politely. "Nashville, Mr. Daniels. I was attending the convention with Jordan."

Drake's eyes widened, and then he nodded slowly. "I see. I'm sorry. I had no idea the two of you were—"

"We weren't. Not then, at any rate. This is a fairly recent... development," Brady said truthfully.

"I see." Drake appeared lost for words.

Belinda appeared at Brady's side. "Is there a reason why Brady is standing here without a drink?" Her eyes sparkled with amusement.

Drake arched his eyebrows but didn't respond. "What can I get you, Brady?"

Brady glanced at the rows of bottles. "Two glasses of the rosé would be perfect." He recalled Jordan's choice of wine when they'd had dinner.

Belinda chuckled. "He still drinks rosé, huh? Nice to see some things don't change." When Brady gave her an inquiring glance, she smiled. "Any time we went out together in our final year at college, either to a party or a bar, Jordan had no interest in beer. He always preferred wine, especially rosé." She waited until Drake handed him the two glasses, then accompanied him away from the drinks table.

"What was Jordan like in college?" Brady was trying to picture him, but what kept coming into his mind was Jordan in his tight jeans, the day he'd visited Brady. Jordan was still talking animatedly with the kids, his eyes bright.

"Focused." Then she grinned. "Drake used to say he was too focused, so *his* way to get Jordan to loosen up a little was to throw a guy in his path."

Brady laughed. "Did it work?"

Belinda smothered a loud chuckle. "Sometimes they'd date for all of three or four weeks; Jordan would decide his grades were slipping, and adios, boyfriend." She studied Jordan for a moment. "He always knew what he wanted, and he wasn't afraid to put in the hours of studying to make it happen. I just think that sometimes, what he *really* needed was…." That intense gaze didn't falter.

Brady was intrigued. "What?"

Belinda sighed. "Someone to love. To be a goof with. To show him that studying wasn't everything. That it was okay to share moments of… intimacy with someone." She flushed. "By then, I already knew I wanted Drake in my life, so maybe that colored my thinking. But Jordan never let anyone get really close." Belinda blinked. "I've known you all of five minutes, and yet here I am, sharing confidences with you."

Brady had wondered about that himself. "Maybe I've just got one of those faces that inspires trust," he suggested.

Belinda shook her head. "It's not that. It's the way you looked at each other when you were standing on my doorstep." She smiled. "I was watching through the window. The two of you looked… good together. Like you fit. So maybe there's hope yet."

"Hope?"

Belinda looked across at Jordan. "That he's found someone who completes him. Heaven knows, it needed to happen." Then she drew herself up. "Forgive me. I shouldn't comment on your relationship."

Brady smiled, though inwardly his heart skipped a beat. A relationship with Jordan. What wouldn't he give for that? Not that he was under any illusions. Such a liaison would only lead to complications neither of them needed.

That didn't stop him from wanting more, however. The heart was *not* a logical organ.

He had no clue what madness seized him, but he couldn't stop the words from escaping.

"Jordan is… amazing. I've gotten to see what lies beneath the surface, and there's so much more to him than I imagined. And the more time I spend with him, the more I see."

Belinda glanced over his shoulder, and then Jordan was there, his warm, spicy cologne announcing his arrival long before Brady felt Jordan's hand at his back.

"I thought I'd better get over here, seeing as my drink never made its way to me."

Brady chuckled and handed him the glass. "And you're clearly dying of thirst."

"That would be my fault," Belinda said with an apologetic glance. "I kept him talking."

"Should my ears be burning?" Jordan's eyes sparkled.

Brady's gaze met Belinda's, and they both smiled.

Belinda patted Jordan on the arm. "If you'll excuse me, I'll go make sure everyone has a drink." She walked off toward a couple standing by the window, looking out at the yard.

Jordan leaned in close. "You okay?"

Brady slowly turned his head to look Jordan in the eye. "I'm good. And I like Belinda. Drake, on the other hand, seemed a little surprised to see me."

Jordan sighed. "Which means at some point this evening, he'll corner me, dying to know more." His hand was still resting against Brady's back, and the intimacy of his stance set up a fluttering in Brady's belly.

Before he could give himself time to change his mind, Brady shifted even closer and whispered, "Want to really give him something to talk about?" He cupped Jordan's cheek and moved in for a kiss.

Jordan stilled for a moment but then seemed to melt under his touch, and he realized with a shock that Jordan was returning the kiss.

Oh my God.

Chapter Fourteen

JORDAN hadn't seen the kiss coming, but *God*, it felt good. Awkward, with a glass in one hand, but so damn good. Feeling Brady's warmth through the thin shirt, his hand, so gentle on Jordan's cheek, his lips, soft as silk against Jordan's…. It was an intoxicating moment, one he didn't want to stop.

What surprised him was the thought that flitted through his brain.

Please, don't let this be just for Drake's benefit.

Because that would really suck. What was even more of a surprise was how badly Jordan wanted it to be more than just an act.

But like all good things, it had to end sometime. When they parted, Brady's eyes were huge. "Wow."

Jordan scanned his face, searching for some sign that this was real. "I like the way you kiss."

Brady smiled, his cheeks flushed. "Funny. I was about to say the same thing." He cleared his throat and stepped back with a glance around them. "Sorry. I'm not usually into public displays."

"Don't apologize on my account." Jordan grinned. "I have no complaints whatsoever." It wasn't like anyone was staring at them, thank God. He sipped his wine, then sighed. "Good choice, by the way." What he really wanted to say was "Why did you kiss me?" Only, he was afraid he wouldn't like the answer.

"Uncle Jordan, who is this?" Dawn appeared at Jordan's elbow, gazing directly at Brady, her eyes bright. Marty joined her.

Jordan shook his head. "We really need to work on your tact. And this is Brady. He's my... boyfriend." The word tasted strange on his lips, yet not unpleasant. He turned to Brady. "This is Dawn and Marty. They're both pests, so you've been warned."

"Hey!" Dawn hit him on the arm.

"And that will be quite enough of that, young lady." Belinda appeared behind her. "What did I say?"

Dawn rolled her eyes. "If we don't behave, we have to go to our rooms."

Jordan loved the typical teenage reaction.

"What's so bad about that?" Marty whispered as Belinda walked away from them. "At least I can play my games there." He glanced around. "It's just old people in here."

Jordan gave him a mock glare. "Well, thanks for that." Beside him, Brady was chuckling.

Marty's eyes widened. "Not you, Uncle Jordan." He gave Jordan a shy smile. "It's great to see you." He gazed at Brady. "So, how long have you been dating? One of my friends at school, his older brother just got married to a guy. I think it's cool."

Brady appeared utterly charmed by the kids. "Not long." He took Jordan's hand in his. "I'm glad Jordan asked me along for the weekend."

Jordan was getting used to the little touches, the intimate gestures. He squeezed Brady's hand, holding on to it, and Brady's eyes shone, his lips parting slightly.

Jordan's heartbeat sped up at the unexpected reaction. *That was real.* That was for him.

Dawn disappeared for a moment, then reappeared clutching a large tray. "Here, try some of these." She leaned closer. "I'd avoid the chicken wings if I were you. They're sticky. But the hogs in a blanket are great. The sausage is spicy. I helped make the crab cakes and dip too."

"Which is a good reason to avoid *them* too," Marty said with a gleam in his eye. "Unless you really want a trip to the emergency room."

Dawn glared at her brother. "Hush, you, or I'll tell Mom why we only have *twenty* miniburgers instead of twenty-five."

Marty responded with a glare of equal force. "You wouldn't."

Dawn gave a sweet smile that didn't fool Jordan for an instant. "Wanna bet?"

Brady laughed. "And to think I missed out on all this by being an only child." He helped himself to a cheese-and-bacon crostini and a miniburger. "Thanks."

"Those crostini look delicious," Jordan commented.

"Here, find out for yourself." Brady held the canapé up to Jordan's lips, smiling. "Excuse the fingers."

Jordan took the morsel in one bite, and Brady's fingers encountered his lips. Brady's eyes grew wide, and Jordan suddenly wished they weren't in a room full of people.

Belinda was back, and Brady hastily retrieved his fingers. "Dawn, you need to make sure everyone gets served. Marty, can you go into the kitchen and pick up the other tray, please?"

Marty nodded and left the room.

"Is this everyone?" Jordan asked, gesturing to the other guests. He didn't recognize anyone.

Belinda shook her head. "There are more coming tomorrow night for the party." She smiled. "You two are the only ones staying here. Everyone else is staying at the Mill House Inn or the Baker House. Mara couldn't make it tonight. Something came up, so she's flying in tomorrow."

"Mara?"

"Mara Stewart. She's on the board of a lot of the charities I work with."

Jordan blinked. "Wow. I didn't realize you moved in such exalted social circles. I'm impressed." He turned to Brady. "Mara's husband is—"

"Tate Stewart," Brady interjected. "He's a billionaire, right? I see him in the financial headlines all the time."

Belinda nodded. "Except lately he's more likely to be seen in the gossip columns. They're in the middle of a divorce, and it isn't pretty. I've gotten to know Mara really well, and I thought she needed a break from all that. When I invited her, she jumped at the chance." Belinda's smile slipped. "She's had a rough ride." She drew in a deep breath. "I'd better see to our guests." She smiled at Brady before heading over to talk to a guy standing with Drake.

Brady watched her. "I really do like her. And those kids... they're great."

Jordan nodded. "I don't get to see them all that often, but I've known them since they were born." He sighed. "Real life gets in the way, I guess. I can count on one hand the number of times I've seen Drake and Belinda in the past ten years or so. Considering how close we were in college, that's pretty bad."

Brady touched his arm lightly. "You just said it. Real life gets in the way. And think about what you've accomplished since you left college. That company. How many people out there have a job because of you? Not just in New York but in other cities across the country. At least you're here. I'm sure they're delighted you came."

Jordan gave him a grateful smile. "And I'm delighted you said yes. I'm glad you're here." When the impulse seized him, he almost denied it, but then he recalled Brady's kiss. *Two can play at that game.* Jordan leaned in and kissed Brady on the mouth, not missing the soft exhale that slipped from Brady's lips.

Kissing him felt... right. Jordan knew he wasn't doing it for appearances' sake—he was doing it because, *God*, he really wanted to kiss Brady.

BRADY broke the kiss first, his breathing ragged. "This is getting to be a habit." The last place he wanted to be right then was in a room full of people. Jordan's kiss messed with his head and stirred him all up inside. Brady had set this particular ball rolling. He knew that, but for Jordan to act upon it made him hope that maybe Phil was right. Maybe Jordan *did* care for him. Maybe there really *was* something there after all.

A cough from behind him had Brady straightening in an instant. What was it about Jordan that made him forget his surroundings, along with any modicum of sense? Brady had *never* lost himself in such a fashion.

"I was going to ask if you wanted a refill, but you seemed... occupied."

Brady didn't miss the note of amusement in Drake's voice.

Jordan cleared his throat. "Thanks, but I've barely touched my first."

Drake arched his eyebrows. "Color me not surprised. You've been too busy with each other to drink." He gave Jordan a stern glance. "Really, you could have told me back in Nashville, you know. That you were already seeing someone? Because it's obvious from watching you two that this isn't a recent development." His stare morphed into a warm smile. "I've never seen you this smitten before, Jordan. It's a good look on you." And with that he left them to attend to his guests.

Brady regarded Jordan thoughtfully. *Smitten?* For a moment he didn't know what to say, but then he retreated into humor. "Wow. I guess we're really good, if that's what he thinks. Maybe Oscar material."

Jordan snickered. "Well, if we keep kissing in front of him...." His gaze met Brady's. "You didn't mind? I didn't overstep the mark?"

"Hey, I started this," Brady said with a smile. "And to answer your question... not in the least. Feel free to kiss me whenever the urge takes you."

Jordan's eyes gleamed. "Dangerous. You never know where an urge will lead you."

"I'll take my chances." Damn, but this conversation was getting him hot.

"Here, try these!" Marty bounced up alongside him, proffering another tray of canapés.

Brady gave a start. "Might I suggest *not* making the guests leap out of their skins?" he said with a grin. He peered at the tray. "These look delicious." He took a circle of pita, on which was piled cream cheese and smoked salmon.

Before he'd even gotten it to his mouth, Jordan helped himself to a couple. "I'll feed myself this time," he said with a smirk. "Seeing as I almost ended up snacking on your fingers last time."

Brady experienced a sudden flash of heat at the thought of Jordan sucking on his finger. *Down, boy.* It had been *way* too long since he'd gotten any. He did his best not to look in Jordan's direction as he ate, because he didn't want to picture those lips elsewhere.

Right on cue, his dick stiffened, and Brady cursed the fact that his jeans were so goddamn tight.

At this rate he wasn't going to get through the weekend. Not without making a move on Jordan, at least, and the way heat was building between them, that was looking more and more like a fait accompli. The prospect of sharing a room sent waves of hot and cold rippling over his skin. Brady could no longer deny that he wanted Jordan—just *looking* at him had Brady's thoughts going off in all sorts of delicious directions—but as to how he made his desires known?

He had yet to work that out.

JORDAN had to admit, so far it had been a great evening. He hadn't expected a sit-down dinner, not for twelve people, but the capacious dining table accommodated all of them. The room itself was spacious, with five huge windows on two sides. At one end of the room was a fireplace, around which were three couches, with an upright piano tucked into an alcove. At the other was the dining area, and the floor-to-ceiling windows opened out onto the patio, with the kitchen off to one side. The vaulted ceiling and pale blue walls gave the room a light, airy feel.

He pushed out a contented sigh. "That was delicious, Belinda."

She laughed. "Alas, unlike the canapés, I cannot take credit for the meal. Everything was catered. There was no way I was going to cook for this number of people, not unless I wanted to spend the entire weekend in the kitchen." She flashed Drake a smile. "That was the first item on the list when it came to planning this get-together, wasn't it?"

Drake gave a rueful laugh. "Oh yes. Otherwise I'm sure she'd have been on the phone to *you* first thing Monday, Morgan," he said, nodding at the guy to Jordan's right.

Laughter broke out at that. Morgan Chambers was a divorce lawyer who practiced on Long Island.

"And we won't be able to repeat this tomorrow evening for the party," Belinda added. "We're expecting another fifteen guests, so we'll have a full house." She grinned at Jordan. "Mara's already dying to meet you."

Brady squeezed his thigh under the table, his lips twitching.

Jordan didn't have to be a mind reader to know what he was thinking. He leaned in close and whispered, "Good thing you'll be here, right?"

Brady chuckled, then straightened his face. "I think it'll be great. I hear she's already on the lookout for husband number three. Your luck might be in."

Jordan narrowed his gaze. "You are *not* helping," he muttered.

Brady grinned.

After coffee, they sat around and listened to Drake playing the piano, mostly easy-listening stuff that formed the backdrop to the conversations. Brady sat quietly for the most part, his hand resting lightly on Jordan's. It was something Jordan could get used to. The kids were in their rooms, keeping out of the way, and Belinda made sure her guests lacked for nothing. She sat next to Brady, telling him about the various charities she was involved in, and he asked lots of questions, his attention focused on her.

It came as a shock when the other guests began to take their leave, and Jordan realized how late it had gotten. It wasn't long before the house was quiet, with only their hosts, him, and Brady left.

Belinda took a swift look around the room, then smiled. "I'm going to bed, guys. I'll do a cleanup first thing in the morning. No one is expected to turn up here until late in the afternoon, so there'll be plenty of time. And you don't need to get up early, all right? Breakfast will be whenever you surface. There's no rush." She smiled. "I'll make sure the kids aren't too noisy. They're across the hallway from you."

Drake stuck his head around the door. "Good night. Sleep well." He gave Jordan a wicked grin.

Belinda rolled her eyes. "Turn out the lights when you're ready for bed. See you in the morning." She gave Drake a mock glare. "Bedroom. Now. Before you embarrass Jordan and Brady any more than you already have." With a shake of her head, she pulled him from the room by his elbow.

Brady chuckled. "I do like her."

Belinda was the last thing on Jordan's mind right then. He got to his feet and held out a hand. "Ready for bed?" His heartbeat sped up, and he felt like he was in his late teens all over again, about to—

Holy hell. The possibilities that arose in his mind….

Brady regarded him with large bronze-colored eyes, his lips parted. "Sure." The word came out as a whisper. He got to his feet unhurriedly, released Jordan's hand, and went over to switch off the various lamps that stood around the room. When they were in darkness but for the lamplight that spilled from the hallway, Brady stood still.

Jordan didn't want to wait a moment longer. He held out his hand once more, clasping Brady's, and without a word, led him to their bedroom.

Chapter Fifteen

BY the time they got inside the room, Brady was almost vibrating with need. All evening, he'd sat next to Jordan, aware of his scent, the woodsy cologne that always stirred Brady's senses. The memory of the kisses they'd shared only served to ramp up his desire, but he did his best to keep it at simmering point. The fact that Jordan had returned his kiss?

There was Brady's green light right there. If he had the nerve to make that move….

Jordan closed the door and flicked on the light. "Alone at last," he said in a joking tone.

"Thank God," Brady muttered, looping his arms around Jordan's neck and claimed his mouth in a fierce kiss. His heartbeat stuttered when Jordan froze for a second, but then Jordan's hands were on his back, his ass, while his tongue took possession of Brady's mouth, and Brady wanted to shout for joy. *Yes!*

Jordan walked him backward toward the bed, and they both tumbled onto it, their arms around each other, lips still locked in that kiss. God, the taste of him…. Brady wound his fingers through Jordan's hair and held on as Jordan kissed him fervently. The question of whether Jordan wanted this was superfluous when he rolled on top of Brady and began to rock against him, soft sounds pouring from his lips, sounds Brady fed back to him, both of them seemingly lost in a fog of desire.

This had to be a dream, one Brady was afraid would end all too soon. He let go of Jordan's head and went for his shirt, his fingers slipping as he hurried to free the buttons.

Jordan broke the kiss, grinning. "What's your hurry? We have all night." Firmly, he took hold of Brady's hands and brought them to his shoulders. He lowered his head until his lips brushed Brady's, and Brady sighed into a kiss that made his toes curl. Jordan appeared to have lost his previous sense of urgency, his hands stroking Brady's neck and face as they kissed. Brady held on to him, fully invested in the kiss, his heartbeat returning to something near normal.

This was heaven. Languid, sensual heaven. And he didn't want it to end.

JORDAN smiled against Brady's lips as he felt him melt into the mattress. He still couldn't believe this was happening, and his only thought was that it was a moment to savor. *How long have I wanted this?* Long enough that he was going to take his time, to make sure it was good for both of them.

When he was sure Brady was relaxed, Jordan sat up, straddling him. "Undressing a man should never be hurried," he said with a smile as he slowly unbuttoned Brady's shirt. He trailed his fingers down to where a stiff nipple pushed against the soft fabric and brushed over it, loving the way Brady shivered. "Anticipation is half the fun. Slowly unwrapping you, revealing this beautiful body.... Enjoying the sight of you, the way you smell, the feel of your skin...." Jordan slipped his hand under the shirt, seeking Brady's warm flesh, the softness of the light covering of hair on his chest, the taut nipple that he couldn't wait to taste....

Brady closed his eyes and sighed. "Love how your hands feel on me."

Jordan smiled. "Wait until you feel my mouth." With that, he pushed aside the fabric, leaned forward, and closed his lips around a warm, hard little nub. Brady's breathing hitched, and he pressed his hands gently to Jordan's head, holding him there. Jordan was aware of Brady moving beneath him, hips rolling in an almost imperceptible undulation, his chest rising and falling, his fingers brushing over Jordan's scalp. Jordan ran his tongue around the nipple, feeling the flesh pebble, goose bumps spreading over Brady's chest in a slow tide.

"Jordan? Kiss me?"

Jordan didn't hesitate. He brought their mouths together in a gentle fusion of lips and tongues, Brady's hands on his back, rubbing slowly, exploring him. When they parted, Jordan resumed his unveiling, pulling Brady up into a sitting position as he slipped the soft shirt off his shoulders, kissing the bare skin as it was revealed, inch by inch. Brady inclined his head to one side, and Jordan took the hint, slowly kissing his neck, tracing a line with his tongue from his collarbone to his earlobe. A shudder rippled through Brady, and Jordan sucked on the warm skin, Brady's musky scent filling his nostrils. When he paused and straightened, Brady let out a sound that spoke of disapproval.

Jordan laughed quietly. "What—am I not allowed to undress?"

Brady grinned. "Only if I'm the one taking off your clothes. And I got the memo—take my time." He reached up and leisurely began to unbutton Jordan's shirt, his earlier urgency fled.

"When I saw you that afternoon at the spa, I couldn't take my eyes off you," Jordan admitted. The sight of smooth skin, a glimpse of that lean body as he'd undressed, that firm, round ass....

Brady blinked. "When? You weren't looking at me."

"How would you know? You turned your back on me in the changing room." He grinned. "Talk about a delicious view."

Brady let out a low gasp. "You were looking?"

Jordan snorted. "Like you weren't looking at me?" He cocked his head to one side. "Did you like what you saw?"

"God, yes." Brady bit his lip. "I didn't mean for that to sound so...."

Jordan laughed again, then leaned forward and kissed him, a slow, lingering kiss that sent warmth flooding through him. When he straightened, he ran a hand over Brady's chest, and again that delicious hitch in Brady's breath was music to his ears.

This is going to be so good.

Brady resumed his unbuttoning. "You distracted me," he said accusingly.

Jordan leaned closer to brush his lips over Brady's ear. "And just in case you're interested, I really liked what I saw. So much so that I can't wait to see you naked again. Only this time, I get to see all of you. Touch you." He traced the curve of Brady's ear with his tongue. "Taste you." His hands were on Brady's back, stroking the soft skin. "Explore you." And because he couldn't resist, he gently pushed Brady onto his back and left a trail of kisses down his torso, feeling the muscles in Brady's abs quiver beneath his lips. When Jordan reached the waistband of his jeans, he shifted position, kneeling on the floor, and pulled Brady closer to the edge of the bed. Jordan nimbly freed the button and lowered the zipper before tugging at the jeans, his need growing inside him, filling him with heat. Brady wriggled, trying to help him, and finally he was naked.

Tossing the jeans aside, Jordan lifted Brady's legs and kissed him from the soles of his feet to the back of his knees before placing Brady's legs on his shoulders. Brady stretched up, grabbed a cushion, and shoved it under his head, his gaze locked on Jordan.

"Please," he whispered. "Jordan...."

Jordan grinned. "Commando? Were we feeling lucky?"

Brady rolled his eyes. "No—*we* happen to go commando sometimes. Now put that mouth to some good use?" He grabbed his stiff dick—fuck, it was gorgeous, about six inches, thick, and with a vein along the side that Jordan longed to tease with his tongue—around the base and held it upright, presenting it for Jordan's attention.

Like Jordan could ignore *that* invitation.

He leaned forward and engulfed the head of Brady's cock, loving how Brady immediately pushed up with his hips, trying to go deeper. Jordan placed his hands on them, holding Brady down while he took his time licking up the shaft from root to tip.

Brady made a plaintive noise, hips pushing against Jordan's grip.

Jordan chuckled around a mouth full of dick and kept up his slow-and-steady cock worship. He sucked on the head before taking him deep, until his nose was buried in Brady's pubes, the smell of him rich and male. Brady's mix of a growl and a gasp was comical. Jordan slid his lips up and down the shaft, varying his speed and pressure, until Brady was writhing, a constant flow of sounds tumbling from his mouth.

Brady pushed hard on Jordan's shoulders, sending him backward onto the rug, then dove off the bed, going for Jordan's pants, his glistening dick bobbing stiffly as he fumbled with the zipper. Jordan's cock pushed against his briefs, bulging through the opened fly, and Brady was on it, molding his mouth around its girth through the cotton.

Jordan groaned at the heat of that mouth. "God, yes." He ignored the fact that he was lying on his back on the rug, his entire world narrowing to his dick. Jordan freed his shaft, but Brady was already pulling at his pants, removing them, taking his briefs with them in a tangled mess of fabric. Then Jordan arched up off the floor when Brady deep-throated him with ease.

Holy hell. The suction was goddamn perfect. Jordan grabbed Brady's head and held him there while he pumped his hips, sliding in and out of that hot, wet mouth. When Brady pulled free, it was only the knowledge that the kids were across the hallway that kept Jordan from shouting. Instead he resorted to a growl that sounded exactly like Brady's.

"Gimme a sec," Brady gasped, before swinging around to straddle his head. He pushed down on the base of his cock, sliding it between Jordan's lips, and Jordan lost no time in taking him deep. Brady's breath warmed Jordan's dick, Jordan sighed with pleasure when wet heat engulfed him, and then they were both in motion. Brady's hips snapped as he drove his cock deep, while he sucked hard on Jordan's dick, head bobbing, picking up speed. Jordan's hips were engaged in a similar motion as he tilted and pushed up to meet each bob of Brady's head. Jordan grabbed Brady's ass, squeezing the firm cheeks, rubbing his finger over Brady's hole.

Brady forced out a groan around his cock and sucked harder, pulling gently on Jordan's balls. The heat, the friction, the wet sounds that filled the room…. Jordan knew he was getting close, only he wasn't about to shoot his load down Brady's throat.

Jordan released Brady's shaft, sliding his hand up and down its length. "Did you bring condoms?" He hadn't planned for this.

Brady pulled free of his dick, scrambled to his feet, and grabbed his bag from beside the bed. "There's one, I think. I hope."

Jordan chuckled as Brady delved deep into a black bag before triumphantly holding up a single square. "Thank God for that." Before he could say another word, Brady launched himself facedown onto the bed, spread his legs, and tilted his ass.

Jordan laughed and smacked one asscheek. "Subtle. Very subtle."

Brady raised himself up onto his elbows and twisted to stare at Jordan over his shoulder. "Who gives a flying leap about being subtle? Get over here, put that on, and get inside me." He wiggled his ass in invitation, then threw the condom onto the bed. "Come on, because after that it's my turn."

Jordan laughed again. "I guess taking our time didn't work." Then Brady's words sank in. *His turn?* He uttered a silent prayer of thanks.

Brady rolled onto his back and pumped his cock. "Not now. Not when I want you so badly." There was an edge to his voice, the faintest tremor, but Jordan caught it.

He got onto the bed and crawled up Brady's body until their faces were inches apart. "I want you too," he whispered. "And I hate to break it to you, but your turn will have to wait. One condom, remember?"

Brady wrapped his legs around Jordan's waist and locked his arms around Jordan's neck. "Then isn't it a good thing I'm a patient man?" Their lips connected in another leisurely kiss. Jordan slipped his arms beneath Brady, aware of the tension seeping from him, a wave of calm covering them both like a blanket.

Some things couldn't be rushed.

BRADY curved his hand around Jordan's cheek. "Let's take it slow, okay? I want to remember this, remember how it feels to have you inside me."

Jordan nodded. "I can do slow. At least, to begin with." His eyes sparkled. "I don't know how long this is going to last, because I'm already too damn close."

Brady pulled him down into a long, drawn-out kiss, their tongues meeting as they explored each other. When the thought struck him, he froze. "Oh God. Lube. I don't have any. Do you?"

Jordan stilled instantly. "Aw, crap."

"We could make do with spit." Brady didn't much like the idea. Been there, done that, and he still recalled how much it had hurt. But he was willing to try, because this was *Jordan*, for God's sake, and despite making it clear he wanted to be inside Jordan, Brady had no idea if he'd ever get this chance again. He was a realist: he knew that for Jordan, this was just sex. They were there; they were horny… it was a no-brainer.

For Brady, it was way more than that. This was sex with the guy he was in love with.

Jordan scanned his face. "I know this is going to sound really personal, but—"

Brady snickered. "We're naked, we're about to—I think that's about as personal as it gets, don't you?"

Jordan had to concede he had a point. "How long has it been for you?"

Brady got where he was going. He sighed. "Long enough that spit wouldn't cut it."

Jordan cocked his head. "Got any moisturizer in that bag of yours?"

"Sure, but you can't use that. Not with latex."

Jordan smiled. "Just get it, please?" He knelt up, and Brady rolled over to reach toward the side of the bed. He handed Jordan the tube, and Jordan kissed him lightly. "Turn onto your front."

Brady did as instructed, his breathing quickening when Jordan moved behind him, his warm hands on Brady's thighs as he gently spread him. There was the snick of the tube's cap, then a moment later, slick hands pulled his cheeks apart and an equally slick finger sank slowly into him.

"Oh." The sound was torn from him. Brady clutched the comforter beneath him, lying still while Jordan gently fingered him, an unhurried motion accompanied by the sound of Jordan's hand working his own dick.

Brady wanted to look, but somehow it was hotter *not* to see. He closed his eyes and listened to Jordan's breathing as it grew more rapid, the erotic sound of hand on cock matching it. Then another finger slid into him, and Brady moaned with the pleasure of it all.

He tilted his ass higher and was rewarded when Jordan's fingers encountered his prostate. "There. Right there." God, the angle was perfect.

"How you look right now," Jordan said in a low voice. "Pushing back onto my fingers. Getting faster."

Brady rocked back and forth, the heat in him blossoming with every brush of Jordan's fingertips inside him. "Wish it was your cock inside me," he whispered. His body ached for that.

Jordan shifted, his chest pressing against Brady's back, his breath tickling Brady's ear. "And it will be. I promise. Just not tonight." He moved his fingers faster, pushing them deeper. "Believe me, I want to be inside you. I want to be buried in this hot, tight hole."

His words set Brady on fire, and he pushed back harder, riding Jordan's fingers. "I want that too. Want to slide into you, feel you wrapped around my dick." God, he wanted that so badly. "Jordan, I don't think I can take much more." His need was white-hot, his dick aching.

"Me neither."

Brady stilled as Jordan's weight pinned him to the bed, and his hot, bare cock settled between Brady's asscheeks. Jordan rocked his hips, sliding his dick over Brady's hole, and Brady rocked with him as best he could, his own shaft rubbing against the comforter beneath him. Jordan picked up speed, his cock sliding faster, and Brady didn't know which was the more sensual—the friction created by his own shaft against the bed or Jordan's dick sliding through his crease.

The outcome was a foregone conclusion. Brady shuddered and came all over the comforter, and seconds later he felt the warmth of Jordan's load as it met his back and ass.

Jordan kissed his neck and shoulders, his body shaking. "If this is what it's like when we haven't got lube, imagine what it will be like when we do?"

Brady turned his head to claim a kiss, and Jordan didn't disappoint him. He cupped Jordan's cheek and smiled. "I think we're going to need more condoms."

Jordan's face lit up. "I think we're going shopping in the morning." When Brady bit his lip, Jordan regarded him quizzically. "What?"

"I'm just thinking about how to get this comforter cleaned without anyone asking too many awkward questions."

Jordan's eyes widened. "I hadn't thought of that." Then he grinned. "Here's what we do. We give it as good a cleanup as we can. Then tomorrow morning, one of us 'accidentally' spills a cup of coffee there." He lay on his back beside Brady. "What do you think?"

Brady shifted closer until his lips were barely an inch from Jordan's. "I think we'd better hold off on the coffee idea until Sunday. Let's leave ourselves some wiggle room for whatever comes to pass tomorrow." He paused. "That is, if you'd *like* something to come to pass."

Jordan closed the distance between them, kissing him softly. "I'd like nothing more," he whispered. "Did you mean it? About… wanting to be inside me?"

Brady gazed into his eyes. "Are you okay with that?" He held his breath.

God, the heat in those eyes….

"Definitely."

Then Brady forgot all about wet spots and lost himself in a kiss that held so much promise for the day to come.

Once they'd cleaned up as best they could, Brady pulled back the comforter and climbed into bed. He blinked as Jordan went into the closet and emerged with a pillow and blanket, which he then laid on the couch. *He's really going to....*

Jordan gave him a warm smile. "Sleep well." Then he lay down and pulled the blanket over him.

Brady stared at him, lost for words. He'd thoroughly expected Jordan to ask to share the bed, especially after what had just transpired. That Jordan hadn't was something of a shock....

Then Brady reconsidered. *He's not pushing himself on me. He's giving me space.* The realization only served to confirm what he already knew: he wanted to hold on to Jordan for as long as he could.

Brady pushed aside the one thought that niggled at him.

What happens when this weekend is over?

Brady didn't want to think that far ahead, especially when he suspected his heart was about to be broken.

Chapter Sixteen

BRADY opened his eyes, aware of the sound of birdsong and sunlight. He reached for his phone to check the time. Too damn early. Brady rolled onto his side and gazed over at the couch. Jordan lay fast asleep, almost hidden beneath the blanket, only the top of his head visible.

Brady smiled. Jordan made the cutest little snores.

He stretched and sat up, glancing at the covers. The comforter didn't look the worse for wear, thank goodness. Warmth curled through Brady's body as he recalled the previous night, but as he lay there, playing their hot encounter over and over again in his head, unease unfurled in his belly.

He said he wanted me too. But would he have made a move if I hadn't... launched myself at him? Then there were the mutual blowjobs, the shameless manner in which Brady had offered up his ass.... *Did I go too far?*

One thing was certain. He couldn't lie there and torture himself with such thoughts.

As quietly as he could manage, Brady eased himself out of the bed, then pulled on his jeans. He rummaged in his bag for a sweater, shivering a little in the cool morning air. A pair of thick socks finished the ensemble, and he was ready to creep out of the room.

The house was quiet, but the aroma of freshly brewed coffee that assaulted his nostrils told another story. Brady walked silently along the hallway into the living room and around the corner to the open-plan kitchen. Belinda stood at the countertop, a cup in hand, staring out at the yard. She turned her head as he approached and smiled.

"Good morning. Seems like I'm not the only early bird around here." Belinda tilted her head to one side. "And I like the look."

It took Brady a second to realize she was referring to his glasses. "It was way too early to be putting in contacts."

Belinda nodded toward the coffee machine. "Want some? Or would you prefer tea?"

"Coffee would be great."

She poured him a cup. "Help yourself to milk, creamer, and sugar, then come sit with me." She went over to the dining table and sat down.

Brady joined her, sipping his coffee as he crossed the floor. "This is good. Just what I need first thing in the morning."

"I take it Jordan is still sleeping?" She smiled. "No change there. He never was much of an early riser. You should have seen him when he had a class first thing. Talk about bleary-eyed." Her eyes twinkled. "Does he still need a bomb under him to get him moving in the morning?"

Brady laughed. "I wouldn't know. By the time I get to see him at the office, he's awake and raring to go. Not that he gets very far without his caffeine jolt."

Belinda stilled. "Okay, I'm a little confused. Drake said he first met you at a conference in Nashville, where Jordan introduced you as his personal assistant. Then *you* told him this weekend that this is a fairly recent relationship. But I've been watching the pair of you. This doesn't feel recent to me. You guys look like you belong together."

Brady took a long drink of coffee. *Hoo boy.* He put down his cup and leaned forward, his hands clasped on the light oak table. "It's a long story."

Belinda leaned back, her cup in her hands. "We've got time."

Hesitatingly at first, he told her how he came to be there, including Jordan's visits to his apartment, the shopping trip, the spa afternoon, and the visit to Jordan's parents. Belinda listened intently, getting up once to refill their cups. When he'd finished, she sighed.

"So you work for Jordan, and you're in love with him," she said simply.

Brady chuckled. "I'm having a sudden case of déjà vu. My neighbor said the same thing." He told her about his conversation with Phil.

She nodded. "I think she's right. When you told me about Jordan turning up on your doorstep, shopping for you, feeding you…. My first thought was 'oh my God, how sweet,' but you know what? There has to be something there for him to act like that." Belinda regarded him closely. "He doesn't know how you feel, does he?"

Brady shook his head. "That was the whole point about this weekend. I was finally going to tell him." He paused. "I just haven't found the right moment yet." Brady stiffened at the sound of a door closing softly. A moment later, Jordan walked into the room, yawning.

Belinda got up, strolled into the kitchen, and returned with a large mug of coffee, which she handed to Jordan, smiling. He glanced at it and laughed. Belinda kissed his cheek. "I figured in this case, actions speak louder than words. And now that you're both up, I'll start breakfast. Eggs, bacon, and pancakes are on the menu." She left them and reentered the kitchen, humming to herself.

Jordan joined Brady at the table. "Hey. I wondered where you'd gone to." He fell silent, and the sudden lull felt awkward to Brady, reinforcing his earlier unease.

Brady smiled. "I was lured out of the room by the scent of fresh coffee," he lied. When Jordan returned his smile but said nothing, he couldn't bear the quiet any longer. "Hey, Belinda, can I do anything to help?" He got up from the table and went into the kitchen.

She grinned. "Are you any good at making pancakes?"

Brady flexed his fingers. "*Now* you're talking. Pancake-making is one of my superpowers."

"And he has many, believe me."

Brady turned to find Jordan standing by the countertop, sipping coffee.

Belinda chuckled. "Wow. I can see why you'd want to keep this one." She winked at Brady. "The bowl's in that cabinet over there. Flour, baking powder, and sugar are in the cabinet above, the milk is in the refrigerator, and the eggs are in that basket by the window. Dazzle me." She continued breaking eggs into a smaller bowl.

"I could deal with the bacon," Jordan volunteered.

Belinda snorted. "Not unless your cooking skills have improved vastly in the last eighteen years."

"Hey, I can cook," Jordan protested.

Brady snickered. "You forget, you're talking to the guy who has your meals delivered." He gave Jordan a hard stare. "And I also know that your car drops you off every morning outside a certain... establishment that serves—"

"Okay, okay." Jordan retreated to the dining table, mumbling something about assistants who knew too goddamn much. But the atmosphere had lightened enough that Brady felt more comfortable.

Maybe everything will be okay after all.

He hoped.

BREAKFAST over, Belinda cleared the dishes. "You were right about the pancakes," she told Brady. "They were delicious."

Brady smiled and buffed his nails on his shirt.

"By the way," she said as she brought them more coffee, "I have to pop out this morning to do a little grocery shopping, which wouldn't be necessary if my dear children hadn't decided to serve themselves popcorn and several glasses of milk last night." She rolled her eyes. "Kids. Plus, I have a couple of things I need to get before the party this evening—"

"I'll do the shopping," Jordan interjected.

Brady suddenly remembered that he had an item or two on *his* list. "No, that's okay. You stay here with Belinda and the kids. I'll go."

Belinda burst out laughing. "Okay. We have three options here. One, you both go to the store. Two, one of you goes and one stays. Or three, *I'll* go and you get to make breakfast for those two little locusts I affectionately call children."

Jordan was up off his chair before Brady could react. "I'll go, seeing as I'm the one on the paperwork for the rental car. Where's the list?"

"On the refrigerator," Belinda told him.

Jordan hurried over and grabbed it. "Where should I go?"

"Turn left onto Stephen Hands Path, then make a left onto Montauk Highway. Then take Main Street, North Main Street, before taking Springs Fireplace Road. It's about a fifteen-minute drive to the One-Stop Market. There's a gas station that's closer, but they're pretty limited. The market is your best shot."

"Jordan?" Brady smiled. "Use your phone."

Jordan rolled his eyes. "Oh, *I* get it. First I can't cook, *now* I can't navigate?" He narrowed his gaze. "Just so you know? I'm writing all this down." The twitch of his lips told Brady the truth, however. Jordan wasn't all *that* pissed.

Within five minutes, Jordan was out the door.

Brady stared after him, his stomach churning, unsure what to make of Jordan's mood. *Is he having regrets?* That question sent ripples of disquiet through him. Brady's only regret was that he hadn't had the foresight to pack condoms and lube. And the solitary condom he'd found was only just within its expiration date.

But I didn't come here expecting that we'd—

"What's wrong?" Belinda sat down next to him, her eyes warm and compassionate.

Brady sighed. No way was he about to share what had happened the previous night. He had limits. "He's just a little… different this morning."

She smiled and covered his hand with her own. "You wait. By the time he gets back, he'll be the Jordan you're used to. He just needs to wake up properly." She gazed at him thoughtfully. "And maybe he just needs a little push in the right direction."

Brady shook his head. "I'm not going to push him." *No, I already did that last night.* If anything else was to happen between them, Brady wanted to be sure it was what they *both* wanted.

JORDAN checked the list, then headed to the cash register. There weren't a huge number of items, and it had taken him all of ten minutes to find everything, which was amazing, considering how distracted he was. Waking up to find Brady wasn't there had troubled him—not that he'd anticipated picking up where they'd left off the night before. But his first thought on seeing the empty bed was that he would've liked to have crawled into it and held Brady for a while before they had to get up.

Maybe he got up because he didn't want to face me.

Jordan hoped to God that wasn't the case. The last thing he wanted was to ruin what they had. *Only... would I be happy if things went back to the way they were?* He liked the Brady who'd emerged from the background during the last month or so, liked the way they connected, interacted. *And last night?* The Brady who'd kissed him with such fervor, who'd been demanding and impulsive and hot as hell?

Jordan didn't want to lose *that* Brady, not even for a second.

As he approached the intersection with Main Street, a familiar sign caught his eye. His heartbeat sped up, and he changed lanes, heading left instead of right. When he switched off the engine in the parking lot of CVS, he knew he'd reached a decision.

Time to do a little more shopping.

"THANKS for that, Jordan," Belinda said as she took the bags from him. "Lunch will be at twelve. Why don't you and Brady go for a walk? You can go to East Hampton Main Beach. It's less than ten minutes' drive from here."

"Are you sure? Maybe we should help you get ready for the party."

Belinda chuckled. "That's what children are for—Mom's little helpers. But seriously, people won't start arriving here until after four, so we have plenty of time to get all the preparations done. Just make sure you're back here for lunch. Oh, and if you turn left along the beach, be careful not to get hit in the head by a stray golf ball." Her eyes sparkled. "Maidstone golf club backs onto the beach." She caught Brady's gaze for a second before walking out of the living room.

Brady knew exactly what Belinda was up to—she was giving him some alone time with Jordan. So much for not pushing. Still, he didn't dislike the idea of a stroll along the beach with Jordan, even if the sky was filled with thick gray clouds. The thermometer on the kitchen wall proclaimed the outside temperature to be sixty-nine degrees, and that wasn't cold by any stretch of the imagination.

"I'd love to see the ocean," he said quietly. When Jordan turned to face him, Brady shrugged. "Not something I've ever gotten the opportunity to enjoy."

Jordan nodded slowly. "Then that's it. Grab your jacket. We're going to the beach."

Ten minutes later they were parking behind a hotel right on the beach. Brady followed Jordan onto the sand and peered up and down the long stretch of beach. There were maybe ten or twelve people, some elderly couples, a family with kids and a very exuberant, bouncy retriever, and a guy walking slowly along, holding out a metal detector.

"Left or right?" Jordan asked him.

Brady grinned. "I'm feeling adventurous. Let's head left."

They walked along the beach at a leisurely pace, Brady's gaze locked onto the waves that crashed onto the shore. There was an energy about it that appealed to him. As much as he loved New York and all that city life had to offer, this was exhilarating.

"So how do you like the ocean?" Jordan asked after they'd been walking for about five minutes in silence.

"I love it." The air hitting his face had a sting to it, and Brady liked the sensation. The ocean had its own smell, and that too was pleasant. "Have you spent much time at the ocean?"

"Not as much as I'd like."

Brady already knew the reason for that. Jordan's time was all tied up with his company.

"Are you enjoying the weekend so far?"

Brady came to a halt and stared at him. "Why do you ask? Does it look like I'm not? So far, it's been great. Some parts of it especially." He left it there. Jordan wasn't stupid.

Jordan bit his lip. "Good to know."

Brady couldn't resist. "Did you find what you wanted earlier? When you went shopping?"

Jordan's face lit up in a wicked grin. "Oh, definitely."

That slow unfurling in Brady's belly was back, only this time, what spread through him was heat.

They resumed their walk, Jordan reaching across for Brady's hand, and the gesture warmed him. "Did you have a good talk with Belinda this morning before I got up?"

Brady nodded. "She really is great."

"What did you talk about?"

He snorted. "You, of course." When Jordan jerked his head to stare at him, Brady chuckled. "Of course we talked about you. I wanted her to dish all the dirt on you from when you were at college. I figured she'd know all your deep, dark secrets." He was enjoying himself.

"Wasn't aware I had any of those," Jordan muttered. He frowned. "What did she tell you?"

Brady couldn't bear to tease him any longer. "She mentioned how hard you studied, and how Drake liked to… distract you by finding you guys."

Jordan laughed. "Oh, he sure did, not that any of them stuck around long."

"Yeah, she mentioned that too." When Jordan arched his eyebrows, Brady gave him what he hoped was a sympathetic smile. "I can appreciate that, not having had much luck in the boyfriend department either."

Jordan blinked. "Now *that* surprises me."

It was Brady's turn to lift his eyebrows.

"What? You're good-looking, intelligent, witty, sexy…. Why would anyone not want to stay around someone like you?"

Brady grinned. "I'm sexy?"

Jordan let out a snort. "You know it."

Brady's grin faltered. "No, actually, I don't, but it's good to know someone thinks of me that way. And maybe I've not had much success because I'm too... picky. I'm not a one-night stand kind of guy. I'm after someone who wants to be... permanent." His throat tightened as the thought flickered through his mind. *And I was kinda hoping you wanted the position.*

"Maybe you've not met the right one yet. I can understand that situation. I mean, look at me. When do I have time for romance?"

It wasn't at all what Brady wanted to hear. Inside his head, a voice was yelling at him to *say something*, but the signals weren't there. "And maybe... we need to get back. We don't want to be late for lunch, right?" He silently cursed himself for his sudden attack of cold feet, arguing that if Jordan had given any indication that he was interested, he'd have said something.

Brady was no fool. A night of blowjobs and frotting added up to one thing only—sex—and he wanted more than Jordan's body.

He wanted his heart too.

Chapter Seventeen

BRADY slipped on the dark green jacket and regarded his reflection.

Jordan came up behind him, smiling. "It still looks amazing on you. That color complements your eyes."

Brady stared at him in the mirror. "You're not too shabby either." Jordan wore a dark blue shirt and black pants. The only thing wrong was that he'd shaved—Brady preferred the five-o'clock shadow that always made Jordan so sexy, almost dangerous. That smooth jawline did have one thing going for it, however—it practically *begged* to be kissed.

Then why not do exactly that?

Brady turned around slowly, stroked his hand over Jordan's cheek, and leaned in to kiss the newly bared skin. Jordan's cologne stirred his senses, and he kissed a trail to Jordan's neck, eager to drink him in.

Jordan made a low sound of approval, his arms slipping around Brady's waist. "This is... distracting."

Brady chuckled against his neck. "I don't hear you saying, 'Stop, stop.'" When Jordan moved his hand lower to gently squeeze Brady's ass, Brady snickered. "Mm-hmm. Yeah. Your mouth says one thing, but your hands say something completely different."

Jordan sighed and let go of his ass. "Unfortunately, there's a party out there, and we're expected."

Brady huffed and straightened. He ran his hand over Jordan's chest, feeling the nipple harden through the soft fabric as his fingertips brushed over it. "Later?"

Jordan kissed him lightly on the lips. "Later," he confirmed. "Now let's go mingle."

Brady gave a final glance at his reflection, then followed Jordan out of their room. Maybe later he'd find the nerve he'd lost out at the beach. Maybe after a couple of drinks, he'd find enough courage to tell Jordan what he felt. Maybe—

Oh, enough with the maybes. Just grow a pair.

The living room was full. Drake was doing his host routine, pouring drinks and talking with his guests, and Belinda was doing the same, circulating with a tray of champagne flutes and chatting. The air was filled with lively conversations and unobtrusive background music. Brady noted the kids were nowhere to be seen.

"Oh. Someone I know." Jordan smiled. "I had no idea he'd be here."

Brady's stomach clenched a little at the sight of that happy expression, but then he pushed down hard on his pang of irrational jealousy. He knew better. "Then why don't you go say hi, and I'll get you a drink?" He patted Jordan's arm. "How about a glass of champagne?"

Jordan nodded. "Then come join me. I'd like to introduce you to Miles." He headed for the window, where a tall, slim man was talking with another guest.

Brady sought Belinda and found her chatting with a woman he recognized instantly as Mara Stewart, every bit as glamorous in real life as she was in photos. He walked up to them, waiting until Belinda was done.

Mara turned her head and stared in Jordan's direction. "Aww, Belinda, for me? You shouldn't have. What a thoughtful gift." She peered intently at him. "Who is he? He's gorgeous."

Belinda laughed. "Sorry, Mara. That's Jordan Wolf, and he's spoken for. So down, girl."

Mara snickered. "As if I'd let a little thing like that stop me. How do you think I got my first husband?" She turned back to face Belinda. "I used my… charms."

Brady decided in that moment that he really didn't like Mara Stewart.

"Trust me, your *charms* will be powerless in this instance. Jordan is gay." Belinda gave a sweet smile, her gaze flickering to catch Brady's. "And his partner is right behind you."

Before Brady could take a breath, Mara whirled around to stare at him. Her makeup was immaculate, as was her carefully coiffured, glossy hair, curling over her shoulders. She showed no signs of embarrassment as she calmly looked Brady up and down.

"So you're the lucky man?"

Brady extended his hand. "Brady Donovan, Ms. Stewart."

Mara took it and shook with a firm grip. "Obviously a man with excellent taste." Her pale blue eyes focused on his, and Brady felt like he was under a microscope.

He gave Belinda a smile. "Two glasses of champagne, please." He had no desire to stay a moment longer to suffer Mara's careful scrutiny. Belinda handed him the glasses, and after giving both her and Mara a brief nod, Brady edged his way through all the guests to the window where Jordan was talking animatedly.

"Brady, this is Miles Hartmann. We met at a conference about four years ago. Miles runs an advertising company on Long Island. Miles, this is Brady Donovan."

Miles gave Brady a nod. "Pleased to meet you. Jordan says this is your first visit to the Hamptons. It's quite something, isn't it?"

Brady smiled politely. "Judging by some of the properties I saw on our way here, it certainly seems to attract those who have a lot of money." The Hamptons had one thing going for it in Brady's book—its proximity to the ocean. Brady loved the idea of living by the water.

"True. Put it this way—*I* couldn't afford to buy a house around here." Miles glanced around him. "And this is a beautiful house, isn't it? So much light. I bet it's awesome to live here in the summer. My wife would love this." He shrugged. "Unfortunately, it's not something she'll ever get to experience." He nudged Jordan. "Surely *you're* doing well enough by now to be able to buy a house in the Hamptons?"

"Who says I want one?" Jordan exclaimed. "And why didn't you bring Michelle with you this weekend?"

"She's visiting her mom in Atlanta. The kids haven't seen their grandmother in ages." Miles glanced over Brady's shoulder and grinned. "Don't look now, Jordan, but *someone* has her eye on you."

Brady stifled a groan. "That would be Mara."

Jordan leaned in closer. "Then isn't it a good thing that I have my boyfriend with me to protect me from her?" And with that, he kissed Brady on the mouth.

The touch of Jordan's lips against his sent all thoughts of Mara from Brady's head. *She can want all she likes.*

"I had no idea." They parted, and Miles smiled at Brady. "Okay, now I'm *really* pleased to meet you." When Brady gave him a speculative glance, Miles's eyes shone. "Don't mind me. I'm just an old romantic at heart. I love it when people find their missing piece. Life is too short to go through it alone." He held up his left hand, where a white gold ring gleamed. "I found mine ten years ago."

Jordan put his hand to Brady's back, a comforting touch that eased him. Brady wanted Jordan to say something, *anything*, that would give him a clue to what was going in his head, but all he did was sip his champagne.

Idiot. This isn't real, remember? Remember why you're here. Play your part.

The sex had been an unexpected bonus, and if Jordan's shopping trip had gone in the way Brady hoped, it would be repeated, but that didn't make it real. This whole weekend was a fantasy.

What was I thinking? Brady gave himself an angry mental shake. *So what if Phil's right and Jordan does feel something for me? That doesn't mean anything can come of it. He said it himself. He has no time for romance, so why am I torturing myself like this?*

A wave of grief rolled through Brady, so acute that it took his breath away for a moment.

"Excuse me," he said to them. "I'll be back in a minute." He couldn't stand there a second longer. Brady took his glass and walked through the guests toward the kitchen. Thankfully the room was empty. Brady drank down half his glass, then refilled it from the bottle that stood in an ice bucket on the countertop. Maybe alcohol would help.

"So, you and Jordan."

Brady had to fight really hard not to groan out loud. He turned resignedly to face Mara. "What about us?" he said with a sigh before drinking more champagne.

"It's serious?" Mara entered the kitchen area and walked past him to the far end where trays of canapés sat. She took a bite from one. "These are delicious."

Brady wasn't sure if he wanted to laugh or lose his temper. Then he remembered where he was. There was no way he would spoil Belinda's party.

"I'm glad you like them, and yes, it's serious."

Mara cocked her head to one side. "But… you work for him, don't you? Belinda was telling me."

Brady frowned. "What does that have to do with anything?"

She huffed. "It doesn't exactly bode well, does it? Sleeping with the boss? Especially as everyone who wants to see Jordan has to go through you first. What are they going to think when it gets around that you're banging the boss?" She smiled, revealing perfect white teeth. "Which, by the way, is terribly clichéd. The boss sleeping with the lowly secretary. It's almost a business institution. Your job is safe, at any rate."

Brady finally reached the breaking point. He took a long drink from his glass, then put it down and faced her head-on. "Let's overlook the fact for a moment that none of this is *any* of your business. What is your problem? Did you want to get into his pants and then you found out he was gay? You're not the first. So now you have a gorgeous guy who won't be remotely interested in you, and that galls you. Instead of moving on, you decide to take your sour grapes out on me. I do understand, however. Your soon-to-be-ex-husband just treated you like garbage, and the fact that he did it all over the pages of any newspaper that would print the story must really hurt. But that's no excuse." By that point he was shaking.

"No, it most certainly is not."

He turned to find Belinda glaring at Mara, her face pale.

Mara swallowed, then opened her mouth to speak, but Belinda held up her hand.

"I asked you here because I felt sympathy for your circumstances. Well, you just used up all my sympathy. Maybe it would be best if you went back to your hotel. I think you're done here."

Mara's pallor matched Belinda's. "My coat is—"

"In the closet in the hallway. I'll see you out." Belinda pressed her lips together, as if to force herself to remain silent.

Mara walked slowly past Brady without a word, for which he was thankful. When they were both out of sight, he leaned against the countertop, his legs still shaking. Brady finished his champagne, then half filled the glass. He still couldn't believe he'd had the nerve to speak out like that, but Mara had gotten him really pissed. He stood there, waiting for the snakes in his belly to stop writhing, letting the champagne dull his nerves.

"Are you okay?" Belinda was back at his side, her arm around his shoulders. "I am so sorry. She had no right to talk to you that way."

Brady sighed. "I stopped listening when I realized that every word out of her mouth took *everything* I feel for him and demeaned it." He took a breath. "I've worked for Jordan for three years, and I guess I've loved him for nearly that long. It's taken me a while to see that, but hey, I got there."

The sound of a throat clearing had him clamming up, and then an icy hand skated down his spine when he realized who was standing at the far end of the kitchen.

Jordan held up his glass. "I came for a refill, and to find you," he said quietly.

Brady scanned his face for some idea of what he was feeling. Jordan seemed... stunned.

Belinda smiled. "Well, looks like you found him. And now I'll go take care of my guests." She glanced at Brady. "Maybe this is a conversation best suited for someplace less... crowded?"

Jordan nodded. "My thoughts exactly. How about we go to our room?"

Brady swallowed. "Okay." There was nothing else to say, now that the cat was well and truly out of the bag.

Time to face the music.

Chapter Eighteen

THE door closed softly behind them, and Jordan couldn't wait a minute more.

"Did you mean what you said? About… loving me for that long?" He locked gazes with Brady, unable to tear away. He'd caught Brady's words as he'd come around the corner into the kitchen, and they'd been enough to bring him to a halt.

He… loves me?

Brady regarded him carefully. "That wasn't the way I intended for it to come out. I'd rehearsed the words in my head so many times, and yet… the timing was never right." He smiled. "I wanted to tell you when we were at the beach, but then you mentioned having no time for romance, and I thought…." Brady chuckled.

"Okay, so I don't think clearly when I'm around you. You mess with my head."

Jordan moved closer. "That works out well. You've been messing with mine for weeks."

Brady blinked. "I have?"

Jordan nodded. "Suddenly the man I thought I knew disappeared, and in his place was this interesting, funny, sexy guy that I wanted to spend time with. A man who stirred something inside me, something I'd never known before."

"And what was that?" Brady's words were a whisper.

Jordan took his hand and led him over to the bed, where they sat down. He took a deep breath. "Remember when we were at my mom's house, in that storm?"

Brady nodded.

"That moment when we were alone, all I wanted to do was hold you. Kiss you."

"You've kissed me a few times since then."

It was Jordan's turn to nod. "And each time, it only reinforces what I know to be true." It was easier than he thought it would be. Brady had already stepped off that particular precipice—all Jordan had to do was follow him. "I love you. I've never felt about anyone the way I feel about you. Maybe that's why it's taken me so long to work it out. But to quote someone not a million miles away... 'Hey, I got there.'"

God, the light in Brady's eyes....

Brady's smile lit up his face. "I think it's time for another kiss, don't you?"

Jordan's heart might have stuttered a little. "I do like the way you think."

Brady removed his jacket, then stretched out in the center of the bed. "Come here."

Jordan joined him, and Brady pushed him onto his back before rolling on top of him. Jordan gazed up into Brady's eyes. "I still can't believe it," he said softly. "This is a dream, right?"

Brady's smile hadn't faltered. "If it is, let's make it a good one." He brought his lips to Jordan's, and Jordan lost himself in the sweetest kiss he'd ever known. He wrapped his arms around Brady's waist, feeling the warmth that radiated from Brady's body. Brady sought his tongue, and Jordan opened for him, deepening the kiss. Brady sighed. "You know we have to go back out there, don't you? We can't just stay in here."

Jordan chuckled. "Why not?"

Brady snorted. "Because anyone with half a brain would know exactly what we're getting up to in here?"

Jordan tightened his grip. "And what would that be?" Not that he disagreed. Brady had a point.

Brady's gaze was smoking hot. "Making love," he said quietly.

Just like that, Jordan's heart soared. "Making love sounds like a wonderful idea, but maybe something best suited to when everyone has left and we're not likely to raise a few eyebrows." He grinned. "And besides, I don't know about you, but I'm hungry."

Brady rolled his eyes. "Then by all means, let's go find you something to nibble on." Jordan moved swiftly, his lips seeking Brady's neck. Brady let out an undignified squeal. "And that doesn't mean me!" He pulled free of Jordan's embrace and scrambled into a sitting position.

Jordan laughed and sat up. "Spoilsport. Okay, let's go find the canapés." He got off the bed and held out his hand. "Come on—*boyfriend.*"

Brady's smiled widened. "I suddenly like that word a whole lot more."

"Why is that?"

Brady stood beside him. "Because now it's real. Now it means something."

Jordan couldn't agree more.

A HUSH fell over the room as Drake called for quiet. He stood by the fireplace with Belinda at his side, both holding glasses of champagne. Marty and Dawn sat on the armchair next to them.

"Thank you, everyone, for joining us this evening to help us celebrate the last fifteen years. We have a lot to be thankful for, most especially our two wonderful children."

Marty guffawed. "That's not what Mom called us this morning."

Dawn elbowed him in the ribs, and everyone laughed. Belinda gave him a mock glare.

Drake chuckled. "When I think back on all the things people told us when we first mentioned starting a family—real gems, such as… having kids is a lot like living in a frat house. Everything's sticky and you're not sure why." A wave of laughter rippled through the room. "Or… with kids, silence is never golden, only suspicious." More chuckles broke out. "And we've learned a lot during the last few years. For any of you contemplating having children, I'll give you one pearl of wisdom. When they get to be teenagers and you want to punish them? Don't take away their iPad, or phone, or whatever the latest technology happens to be." Drake grinned gleefully. "Just take away their charger, sit back, and wait for the batteries to die."

Brady leaned into Jordan as the guests around them laughed. "These days, kids are likely to report a parent who did that for child abuse," he said in a low voice.

Jordan gazed at him with interest. "How do *you* feel about having kids?"

Brady snickered. "Whoa. Slow down."

"I don't mean *now*, obviously," Jordan whispered. "But in the future? Have you ever thought about it?" He had to admit, it wasn't something that lit a fire under him. Other people's kids were great. Having a few of his own was another matter entirely.

Brady bit his lip. "Not really. I guess I'm not the paternal type." He peered closely at Jordan. "Is that a deal breaker?"

Jordan hastened to reassure him. "Not in the slightest."

Brady heaved a sigh. "Thank God." He nudged Jordan's belly with his elbow. "You're being talked about."

"Huh?" Jordan returned his attention to Drake and Belinda, who were staring at him with amusement.

"As I was just saying," Drake said pointedly, "we're especially glad our friend Jordan Wolf could be with us this weekend, seeing as he's known Belinda and I since we first started dating. In fact, us being here is all his fault."

Belinda coughed loudly, and a couple of people snickered.

"Okay, let me rephrase that. Jordan introduced us, so I guess we have him to thank." Drake turned to Belinda with a smirk. "Is that better, honey?"

She gave him a sweet smile. "I'll tell you later when there are no witnesses." When their guests had stopped laughing, her gaze met Jordan's. "Who knows? In a few years' time, we could be in New York, helping Jordan and Brady celebrate *their* anniversary." Her eyes sparkled with mischief.

Jordan erupted into a coughing fit, and more laughter ensued. Brady joined in. "Er, Belinda? That might classify as a cart-before-horse situation." He grinned.

Belinda matched his grin. "Hey, I'll organize it. All you two have to do is be there."

Jordan cleared his throat and raised his glass. "To Drake and Belinda. Happy anniversary, and many more of them." His toast echoed around the room as glasses were raised.

Drake waved a hand in the air. "That's it for the speeches. There's plenty more food and champagne to be consumed, so enjoy yourselves."

Conversations resumed, and the music began playing again in the background.

Brady chuckled. "Neatly dodged, if I may say so," he murmured.

"Who was dodging?" Jordan brushed his lips over Brady's ear, noting the shiver that coursed through him. "Who's to say where we'll be in a few years' time? I have no idea, but I'll lay even money that wherever we are, we'll still be together." He put his arm around Brady's waist and kissed his cheek. "Because I am not letting you go."

"Just so you're aware? That comes across as either really romantic—or very sinister."

Jordan laughed.

Marty bounced up to them with Dawn following him more sedately. "So, Uncle Jordan, does that mean you and Brady are going to get married now?"

Dawn rolled her eyes. "You are such a douche bag. And who says they have to get married? Just because your jack-wad buddy's brother got married to a guy doesn't mean *everybody* has to." She spoke with all the superiority that only a fourteen-year-old girl could nail.

"Excuse me?" Belinda's eyes almost bulged out. "Since when do I let you talk like that in this house?"

Dawn froze. "Sorry, Mom."

Jordan gave her a sympathetic glance but coughed and straightened his features when Belinda glared at him.

"I think it's time you went to your room," Drake said, wandering over to the small group.

"He's talking to us, right?" Brady whispered, and Jordan had to stifle his snort at hearing the hopeful note in Brady's voice. Belinda caught Brady's question, and her lips twitched.

"Night, Uncle Jordan," Dawn intoned. "G'night, Brady. Will you still be here when I get up in the morning?"

"We're not leaving until after lunch," Jordan confirmed.

Marty brightened immediately. "Great. Then tomorrow I'll let you play with my rat, Monty." He left the room with Dawn trudging behind him, calling him a dweeb under her breath.

Jordan couldn't repress his shudder. "Why on earth would I want to play with a rat?"

Brady's eyes were bright. "Aw, rats are cute, especially when they run across your shoulders and try to climb onto your head."

Belinda laughed. "I don't think you're helping, Brady." She glanced down at their glasses. "I'll bring you two some more champagne. After all, you're celebrating too, right?" She walked toward the kitchen.

Brady's eyes met Jordan's. "I guess we are. Does today count as day one, or do we include the last couple of weeks too? Because you started kissing me a while back."

"Only because you kissed me first," Jordan retorted. Then they both started laughing.

Brady shifted closer. "I'm just looking forward to more of those kisses." He leaned until his breath fluttered against Jordan's ear. "Starting tonight."

Jordan's breathing hitched. "Don't move," he muttered. "Stay right where you are."

Brady opened his eyes wide with alarm. "Why? What's wrong?"

"Nothing, but if you move, something's going to be fairly obvious, so you can stay there until things… quiet down."

Amusement danced in those gorgeous bronze-colored eyes. "Oh my."

"And you can wipe that smirk off your face. This is your fault, after all."

"Mine?" Brady blinked. "All I did was mention kissing you."

"It was the thought of what *follows* the kissing that got me… interested."

Belinda returned, carrying a bottle of champagne. "Here you are." She filled their glasses, then gave them both a warm smile. "I really am delighted you two are together—*really* together." Her eyes twinkled. "Enjoy what's left of the party. And if you want to… escape, I won't mind."

As she walked away to talk to her other guests, Brady gave Jordan a hopeful glance.

Jordan shook his head. "Patience is a virtue. Good things come to those who wait." When Brady glanced at the clock above the fireplace, Jordan added, "And a watched pot never boils."

Brady smirks. "You lost this argument as soon as you said 'come.' Now it's all I can think about." He grinned. "I had my patience tested once. I'm negative."

Jordan shook his head. "Is this what I have to look forward to?"

Brady stilled, his hand on Jordan's cheek. "This—and a lot of love. All I can give you."

Jordan could live with that.

Chapter Nineteen

JORDAN closed the bedroom door behind them and heaved a sigh of relief. "That was one long party."

Brady opened his eyes wide. "There was a party tonight?" He kicked off his shoes, Jordan doing the same.

Jordan laughed. "I'll have to apologize to Drake and Belinda in the morning. We weren't exactly very social, were we?" He and Brady had spent the evening talking, the laughter and chatter of the guests reduced to mere background noise. "I hope none of the other guests minded."

Brady let out a chuckle and moved closer. "What guests? I only had eyes for you. Corny, I know, but accurate." He put his arms around Jordan's neck. "I could have spent the whole night just looking at you. I had to keep telling myself that this is really happening."

Jordan could relate to that. "I know. I kept staring at you, thinking, 'This is real. Brady loves me.'" Just saying the words filled him with a lightness that suffused his entire body.

Brady nodded slowly, his gaze locked on Jordan's. "I do." He smiled. "Do I need to say it again?"

"Only if I get to say it back to you."

Brady leaned in until his lips were almost touching Jordan's. "I love you," he whispered.

"God, I love you too." Jordan closed the minute distance between them, fusing their lips in a kiss that sent a slow, burgeoning wave of desire through him. His hands were on Brady's back, moving over him unhurriedly, reacquainting himself with the feel of Brady's body against his.

Brady fed him a soft sigh, stroking Jordan's nape. "How about we pick up from where we left off?"

Jordan smiled. "Hmm. Remind me. Where was that?"

Brady kissed him, then pulled back a little and glanced toward the bed. "Something about… making love?" He took hold of Jordan's hand and led him across the floor. "Because right now, I can't think of anything I'd rather do."

Jordan eased him out of the jacket, then placed it on the armchair beside the bed. "Now, where were we?"

Brady grinned and pushed him back onto the bed, laughing as Jordan gave an involuntary bounce. He covered Jordan with his body, his hands stroking Jordan's head. "Here, I believe." And then he claimed Jordan's mouth in a lingering kiss, exploring him, cradling Jordan's head as though he was something precious.

God, he can kiss. Jordan could envisage spending whole Sunday afternoons with Brady, curled up together on the couch, doing nothing but kissing and caressing.

He pulled Brady's shirt free of his pants and slipped one hand under the fabric to stroke his warm skin, while he cupped the back of Brady's head. Brady broke the kiss to look him in the eyes, as if he was reassuring himself that this was happening, before taking Jordan's mouth in a kiss that made his toes curl. Jordan sought his neck, kissing and sucking the soft skin, and Brady let out a low moan that reverberated through him.

Gently, Jordan eased him onto his back, then tugged at the shirt, baring Brady's torso. He planted one kiss there before shifting to lie on top of Brady, his thigh between Brady's legs, his hands in constant motion as he stroked and caressed him.

Brady threw an arm around Jordan's neck, pulling him deeper into a kiss, then slid his hand lower to unbutton Jordan's shirt. As each inch of skin was revealed, Brady stroked it, trailing his fingertips, exploring him.

Jordan smiled against Brady's lips. "Let me," he whispered, sitting up to remove his shirt. He loved this slow dance, the heat building between them, the way Brady never stopped touching him as he undressed, the desire in Brady's eyes as Jordan leisurely unbuttoned his shirt. Jordan bent over to kiss Brady's newly bared chest, loving how Brady arched up into his touch, biting his lip as Jordan flicked his nipple with his tongue.

Brady pulled himself into a sitting position to free his arms from his shirt, then wrapped them around Jordan's waist, burying his face in Jordan's chest. Jordan cupped his cheeks and tilted Brady's head to kiss him, pausing to stare at him in awe. He wanted to burn every second of this into his memory. Gently, he lowered them both back down onto the comforter, their lips meeting once more, Brady's chest warm against his.

Jordan broke the kiss and rubbed across Brady's belly with a firm hand before moving lower to unfasten his belt. Brady lifted his head to watch as Jordan unzipped his pants, then cupped his nape and pulled him down into a kiss while Jordan slowly rubbed his stiffening dick through his briefs.

Jordan had no intentions of hurrying. He wanted this to last.

BRADY moaned with pleasure as Jordan slipped his fingers beneath the waistband of his briefs, lightly brushing them against the head of his cock. "Why on earth... did I choose to... wear briefs today of all days?" He buried his face in Jordan's neck as Jordan rubbed his thumb under the head, then chuckled as Jordan trailed the tips of his fingers over his belly. He caught his breath as Jordan sat up to tug Brady's pants down, revealing one asscheek, then bent over to kiss it, stroke it, rake across it with his fingernails.

"God, yes," Brady hissed.

Jordan took the hint and got off the bed. He lifted Brady's legs into the air and removed his pants, socks, and briefs. Brady stroked his dick as Jordan undressed, but the sight of Jordan's erection, clearly visible as it pressed against his boxer shorts, was too much to ignore. Brady sat up, grasped the waistband, and slid them down over Jordan's hips, coming face-to-face with a thick, solid cock that rose up as if to greet him.

Like Brady could resist that.

He wrapped one hand around Jordan's shaft, and in one swift move, took him deep, squeezing and stroking Jordan's ass as he worshipped him with his lips and tongue.

Jordan groaned, his hands resting on Brady's head as he thrust gently. He let out a gasp. "Let me take off my socks before we go much further."

Brady chuckled around his cock and pulled free. He shifted higher on the bed until his head hit the pillows, knees bent, loving the sight of Jordan crawling up to lie between his spread legs. When Jordan kissed his neck, his mouth, his chest, Brady was in heaven. Jordan's scent surrounded him, and the heat of his dick against Brady's sent a shiver of anticipation through him.

"Supplies?" he murmured.

Jordan grinned. "Under the pillow."

Brady had to laugh. "I love a man with initiative." Then all such practicalities were swept away when Jordan shifted lower to lap the head of Brady's cock, his hand cupping and gently squeezing Brady's balls. When Jordan rubbed over his pucker with a single finger, that was all the impetus Brady needed to grab the lube. He placed the tube and the condom within Jordan's reach.

Jordan snickered. "I take it that's a hint."

Any response Brady might have made was lost when Jordan rolled his ass up off the bed and kissed his way down Brady's shaft and over his sac before spreading his cheeks and teasing Brady's hole with his tongue.

"Oh God," Brady croaked, placing his hands firmly on Jordan's head, keeping him there. He couldn't hold back the noises that poured from his lips as Jordan continued to worship his ass. Brady covered Jordan's hands with his own, craning his neck to watch, his whole body tingling as if every cell responded to Jordan's touch.

God, could this be any hotter?

A moment later he had his answer when Jordan slid a finger into his ass. Brady moaned as Jordan alternated between tongue and fingers before swallowing his dick. Brady pushed up off the bed, seeking more of that heat. Jordan's mouth on his dick and his finger in Brady's ass were a heady combination.

When it all came to an end, he wanted to groan in frustration. Then he realized two could play at that game.

Brady pushed Jordan onto his back, heaved his ass up off the bed until Jordan was almost folded in half, then speared that inviting tight hole with his tongue. Jordan clutched his knees and groaned as Brady enjoyed every second of the rim job he'd been waiting for all day. When Jordan was nice and loose, Brady grabbed the lube, slicked up a couple of fingers, and slowly pressed them into Jordan's hot channel.

"So who gets to go first?" he said with a grin, moving his fingers in and out of Jordan's now-slick ass.

"Who fucking *cares* as long as one of us makes a decision?" Jordan said with a groan. He reached for the condom and tore it open.

Brady made his mind up. He dropped onto his back, grabbed his knees, and pulled them up toward his chest. "In me," he begged.

Jordan nodded, and Brady held his breath at the sight of Jordan covering his shaft. Brady was on fire, unable to take his eyes off the heavy cock that was about to enter him. He shivered at the first touch of Jordan's dick against his body. Jordan pushed—slowly, so slowly—until Brady was full to the brim.

God, he'd missed this. But what made it all the more exquisite was that this was *Jordan*, and this moment had been years in the making.

Fully seated, Jordan lowered himself until their lips met in a tender kiss. Brady curled one arm around his neck, holding on to him as the kiss spun out, and Jordan stilled inside him. Then he began to move, a gently rocking motion while they kissed, Brady's hand on his nape, the other between their bodies as he languidly worked his shaft. His breathing quickened, keeping pace with Jordan's thrusts as he, too, picked up speed. Jordan hooked his arms under Brady's knees and buried his shaft to the hilt, their kisses growing in urgency.

Jordan slowed down, propping himself up on his hands to gaze at Brady, lips parted, his dark eyes locked on Brady's, his hips moving in a gentler rhythm. Brady nodded, content with the change in pace, anxious to hold on to the delicious sensations that rippled through his body for as long as possible. It wasn't long, however, before he wanted more.

Brady reached down to grab Jordan's ass with both hands, pulling him tight against his body. Jordan got the message and moved faster, until he was driving his cock deep and Brady was fighting hard not to cry out loud with sheer joy as Jordan propelled them both closer to orgasm. He buried his face once more in Brady's neck, hips snapping, flesh slapping against flesh.

"Close," Jordan gasped out before kneeling up and gripping Brady's shoulders. He brought their foreheads together, their breath mingling as he held on, sliding in and out with short, rapid thrusts, until Brady knew he was about to come. Brady tugged hard on his dick, unable to hold back his cries as wave upon wave of pleasure broke over him, aware of nothing but the warmth that coated his belly, the throb of Jordan's dick inside him, and Jordan's lips against his.

JORDAN closed the distance between them, their bodies slick with perspiration as he held Brady against his damp chest, his hand tenderly cupping Brady's face as they kissed, aware of his heartbeat returning to near normal. Brady's breathing had slowed too, his eyes shut, his hands moving in unhurried, deliberate circles on Jordan's back. Neither of them spoke—words would have been superfluous—and the minutes ticked by in comfortable silence.

Brady was the first to break the kiss and the quiet. He stroked Jordan's cheek and sighed happily. "I don't want to move."

Jordan chuckled, then grimaced at the slickness that glued them together. "Not an option. So let's grab a quick shower, and then we can get right back to—"

"Cuddling," Brady interjected. "In bed. Both of us. All night."

Jordan couldn't help smiling. "Okay, cuddling." The thought of falling asleep with Brady in his arms was a pleasant one.

"Followed by more lovemaking," Brady added. "Whenever the mood takes us."

"And you can see the mood taking us?"

Brady beamed. "Definitely. My dick has a date with your ass."

"Then I'd better leave the lube and condoms within reach."

"Smart man."

Another thought occurred to Jordan. "If you wake up before me again in the morning, don't get up, please?"

Brady shook his head. "I had no intentions of doing any such thing. I want to make this weekend last as long as it can. That includes making the most of time spent in bed." His eyes sparkled in the lamplight.

Jordan knelt up and smacked his ass, making him yelp. "Bathroom. Before it gets much later."

Brady clambered off the bed, picking up the soiled condom from where Jordan had placed it on the nightstand. He rubbed his ass as he entered the bathroom, muttering about bossy boyfriends.

Jordan sat for a moment, Brady's words still in his mind. He had a feeling Sunday would slip through their fingers, as much as they tried to hold on to it. Then it would be back to New York, work—and very different circumstances.

Chapter Twenty

BRADY did *not* want to get up.

Not that he had to move just yet. It was way too early and the rest of the house was silent. Add to that, he was warm, he was comfortable, and Jordan was curled around him, his arm around Brady's waist.

Heaven.

Brady could have stayed like that forever, except he knew Monday morning was coming up fast, hurtling toward them like a freight train. He wasn't usually one to dread work, but the thought of going back made him slightly uneasy.

The feeling of warm lips on his back was a welcome intrusion.

"Good morning." Jordan tightened his arm around him, stroking his chest. "I could get used to this."

Brady sighed. "Me too."

Jordan stilled his hand. "And that was far too heavy a sound for this morning. What's wrong?"

It was on the tip of his tongue to deny anything was wrong, but Brady had learned a lot about Jordan during the past month. Such as, keeping his feelings to himself didn't work—Jordan seemed to possess an uncanny knack of sensing when Brady had concerns. Besides, surely it was better to voice his fears *before* they arrived at the office on Monday morning?

No time like the present.

Brady rolled over to face him. "What happens tomorrow morning?" he asked quietly.

Jordan blinked and rubbed his eyes. "Same thing that always happens on Monday—work."

Brady rolled his eyes. "I didn't mean that. I meant our working relationship. Things have changed, haven't they?"

Jordan regarded him steadily for a moment, then propped himself up on his elbow. "Keep talking."

"How are we going to do this? What will people say?"

Jordan frowned. "Okay, where is this coming from?"

Brady sat up in bed and leaned back against the pillows, hands clasped in his lap. "Mara said something that got me thinking, that's all."

"Mara?" Jordan widened his eyes. "What on earth did that bi—*woman*—say to you? And why the hell would you pay attention to a word she said anyway?" He scowled. "Belinda was still pissed last night, hours after she'd left."

Brady laid his hand on Jordan's arm. "She just… *suggested* word would get around the company that we're—"

Jordan sat up with a jolt. "What if it does? What's wrong with that?" His voice softened as he leaned across to cup Brady's chin. "Brady?"

His touch was reassuring. "You don't see it as an issue?"

Jordan smiled. "Why should it be an issue that we're in a relationship?"

His relaxed manner finally seeped into Brady, easing his tension. "You really don't think staff will mind?"

Jordan laughed. "How much time do we spend working together? I don't think it would come as any great surprise to anyone. And it's not as if us being in a relationship will adversely affect what happens in the office. We make a great team. That won't change." He smiled. "You never know—we might work even better together." Jordan suddenly grabbed hold of Brady's legs and tugged hard, pulling him farther down the bed, Brady squealing, protesting, and laughing all at the same time. Then Jordan leaned over him, caressing his cheek. "It'll be fine. I promise." He placed a tender kiss on Brady's forehead, then his nose, finally reaching his lips before lying on his side, head supported by his hand, gazing at Brady, his eyes warm. "Feeling better?"

Brady sighed and nodded. "I'm sorry. I just didn't see how we could continue as before."

Jordan regarded him thoughtfully for a moment. Then to Brady's surprise, his expression grew serious. "You know what? Maybe you're right. Maybe it's foolish to assume we could just carry on as normal."

The change in mood chilled him a little. "What… what do you mean?"

Jordan rolled onto his back and stared at the ceiling. "I've been ignoring the signs for long enough. Maybe it's time I followed advice."

Panic surged through him. "Okay, now you're scaring me."

Jordan groaned. "God, I'm such an idiot." He pulled Brady into his arms, tilting his chin so he looked Brady in the eye. "I'm sorry for worrying you. Don't be scared. It's nothing that you're not already aware of." He stroked Brady's cheek. "You take such good care of me. You watch my diet. You deal with a lot of stuff so that I don't have to. But the bottom line is, my doctor is concerned about my blood pressure. It's too high."

Brady stilled. "You've never mentioned it."

"Because I thought I was coping. Well, apparently I'm not, according to Dr. Peters at least."

"Exactly how high are we talking?"

"Not high enough to warrant me taking meds for it. Well, not yet at any rate. He'd prefer prevention rather than cure. He's suggested I cut back on my office hours, my business trips. Spend a little time at the gym." Jordan regarded him thoughtfully. "Maybe I should do just that."

Brady knew that expression. "So what's your plan? I'm right, aren't I? You *do* have a plan."

Jordan nodded slowly. "I propose taking on a chief operating officer. Not to replace me, you understand, but to share the workload. In essence, we'd share the running of the company. That would mean less stress for me, which in turn would make my doctor a very happy man. But the COO would have control of the company when I'm not there." He smiled. "Let's face it. A lot of what I do could equally be done from home via a computer."

"Great," Brady said gloomily.

Jordan's brow furrowed. "You don't like the idea of me being under less stress?"

"*That* part I love. What I *don't* like is the you-spending-less-time-in-the-office part. I like working with you."

Jordan's eyes gleamed. "And just who do you think I had in mind for the role of COO?"

It took a moment for his words to sink in. "Me?"

Jordan laughed. "Brady, you're perfect for the job. You're already acquainted with every aspect of the company. You already liaise with all the department heads. You know how the company functions on a day-to-day basis." He snickered. "You're already doing the job of a COO. Maybe it's time your paycheck reflected that." He peered intently at Brady. "I'm beginning to think having sex scrambled your brains. Surely you realized you were the only candidate for the position." Jordan smirked.

Brady narrowed his gaze. "I can envisage a lot of rumors flying around if the boss suddenly starts dating his PA who subsequently becomes the COO. You can't do that, not in today's climate. You'll still have to conduct interviews, you know."

Jordan nodded. "And what if I told you I don't envisage those rumors? I know my staff, their capabilities. That includes yours. And I'm not worried, especially as I already know how your appointment would be received. I'm not the only one who sees what an asset you are. Granted, the relationship might surprise them—but then again, maybe not."

Brady's head was spinning. *He's serious.*

"We'd also need to interview to find a new personal assistant," Jordan added. "That will be a tough one."

"Why?"

"Because whoever replaces you will have to be *at least* as capable as you. Someone who can be relied upon to keep things running while we're away from the office."

"While *we're* away?" Brady grinned. "You *have* been thinking about this, haven't you?" His initial shock was ebbing away with every word from Jordan's mouth.

Jordan laughed and tugged Brady to lie on top of him. "Well, if *I* can work from home, then I see no reason why *you* couldn't do the same thing. Providing, of course, that 'home' happens to be the same place for both of us." He locked gazes with Brady, his hands resting lightly on his back.

Brady arched his eyebrows. "That sounds very much like you asking me to live with you," he said slowly.

Jordan nodded. "There's room for both of us in my apartment. Or if you like, we could find a new place. But I want us to be together. And much as I like your apartment, it's not big enough for two, is it?"

Brady couldn't deny that.

"I know it feels fast, but…." Jordan stroked up and down his back. "I don't want to waste any more time."

"Neither do I." Brady closed the gap between them and kissed him. "And speaking of wasting time… we don't have to get up right now, do we?"

Jordan's smile lit up his face. "Actually, I was thinking about an early morning ride."

Brady snickered. "Well, your doctor *did* say to take more exercise. And you'll be the one doing the riding."

Breakfast could wait for another hour. Or two.

"WHERE'S Jordan disappeared to?" Belinda asked as she poured Brady another cup of coffee. Breakfast was over, Drake was in the yard practicing his golf putts, and the kids were playing with Marty's pet rat. Brady thought it amusing that as soon as Monty put in an appearance, Jordan suddenly announced he had an urgent call to make and retreated to their room.

Brady laughed. "I think Monty scared him off."

Belinda chuckled. "Not really a surprise. He's had an aversion to rats since we were in college. We watched this seventies horror movie about a boy who had an affinity for rats. I think Jordan watched the entire movie through his fingers." She glanced across the room at the kids. "Marty? Put Monty back in his cage before Jordan comes back."

Marty's face fell. "Aw, Mom. I wanted to show Uncle Jordan how Monty runs up my arms and across my shoulders."

Belinda narrowed her gaze. "While *I* can appreciate what a little star Monty is, Jordan will not feel the same, believe me. Cage. Now."

Marty pouted, lifted Monty from Dawn's knee, got up off the couch, and trudged toward his room. Dawn grinned gleefully.

"And before you start gloating, young lady, I just peeped into your room. Go clean up your mess."

"Mom," she whined, but fell silent when Belinda stared at her with arched eyebrows. "Going now." She followed her brother.

Brady laughed. "Wow. You're good."

She chuckled. "They know better than to argue. They're well-trained." She poured another cup of coffee and sat with him at the table. "I hope you had a good time this weekend."

"I had a wonderful time," he assured her. "It was great getting to know you and your family."

"Maybe Jordan will bring you back soon, rather than waiting the customary couple of years between meetings," she said, her eyes twinkling. "You could work on him."

He laughed again. "Well, based on our conversation this morning, you might find him visiting more frequently."

Belinda snorted. "I'll believe that when I see it. Sometimes I think that man lives in his office."

Brady grinned. "Miracles do happen, you know."

Belinda peered at him closely. "Now I'm intrigued." Before she could continue, Jordan entered the room, glancing around him.

Brady snickered. "You're safe. No more Monty. Have you finished your 'call'?"

Jordan gave a broad smile. "Actually, yes." He turned to Belinda. "I'm sorry, but we'll be leaving a little earlier than I'd planned."

Her face fell. "Aw. I was hoping you'd stay for lunch."

Brady's stomach clenched. He didn't want to go home. The weekend had been a precious bubble of time that he wanted to hold on to for as long as possible.

"As much as I love the idea, I had something else in mind." Jordan's gaze alighted on Brady. "Something just for the two of us."

And just like that, sunlight poured into him, flooding Brady with warmth. "Really?"

Jordan nodded. "I don't know about you, but I'm not ready to go home right this minute. And there's somewhere I'd like us to visit. That's what the phone call was about. Everything's arranged."

"That's so sweet." Belinda sighed. "By all means, go spend time together. That's way more important than having lunch with us. You two must have a lot of things to talk about."

Jordan's dark eyes were still focused on his. "Oh, we do." Then he walked over to where Brady sat, bent down, and kissed him softly on the mouth.

Brady liked those kinds of conversations. He gazed up at Jordan. "So where are you taking me?"

"It's a surprise. And the sooner you're packed, the sooner you'll find out."

Brady rolled his eyes. "You're such a tease." A second later, he was hurrying to their room, still hearing Belinda and Jordan's laughter behind him.

Chapter Twenty-One

"WHERE are we headed?" Brady asked, staring out the window. He hadn't taken his eyes off the ocean ever since they'd joined the Montauk Highway.

"To Montauk." Jordan took a right. "This is the old highway." It was even closer to the shoreline. "What you see to your left is the Hither Hills State Park." The canopy of trees was a gorgeous mixture of fall colors.

Brady sighed. "It's so beautiful here." At last he turned away to look in Jordan's direction, smiling. "I could live here. And before you say a word, yes, I know it's not practical, but I don't care. There's something about the ocean that I find…."

"Fascinating? Compelling?" Jordan could understand that. His best memories as a child were of vacations spent by the sea.

"Any of those will do." Brady peered through the windshield. "Want to tell me where we're going yet?"

"Here." Jordan turned right off the highway. "Welcome to Gurney's Montauk Resort and Seawater Spa."

Brady laughed. "Another spa afternoon? You're spoiling me."

"Actually, I was planning on spending the night. That is, unless you have any objections to taking another day away from the office?"

"Another—"

"And before you tell me that the company couldn't possibly manage for another day without either of us, let me inform you that I've already emailed a schedule to the heads of department."

Brady snorted. "What—you mean the schedule *I* sent you last week, so you'd be ready for Monday?"

"Exactly. There's nothing urgent planned for tomorrow, and they'll cope just fine." Jordan pulled into a parking space and switched off the engine. "Any more questions?"

Brady chuckled. "Just one. Where is Jordan Wolf and what have you done to him?"

Jordan burst into laughter. "Out of the car. Before I change my mind."

They got out, and Jordan led him to the resort's reception desk. Once he'd registered them, they headed for their room. Jordan held his breath as he opened the door and stood aside to let Brady enter. His soft cry was everything Jordan had anticipated.

"Oh. This is… amazing." A wide, comfortable-looking bed stood against one wall, but Jordan knew what had captured Brady's attention were the windows at the far end, along with the door that opened out onto a veranda and the sandy beach beyond. A pale blue couch sat by the windows, perfect for lying on to stare at the clear sky, or better still, for two to lie together, snuggled up, listening to the crash of the waves on the shore through that open door.

"Do you like it?" As if he needed to ask.

Brady's eyes shone. "It's perfect."

"We've just got time to have a drink in the lounge before we have lunch." Jordan smiled. "We have all afternoon to spend in here, if we want to. Or we can go for a walk on the beach, whatever you want."

"Yes," Brady replied promptly.

"Yes?"

He grinned. "All of the above, please." Brady moved closer, cupped Jordan's face in his hands, and kissed him, taking his time. When they parted, he smiled. "More of that after lunch."

Jordan chuckled. "In that case, we won't be needing dessert."

This had to be one of the best impulses he'd ever had. Then he reconsidered. No, the best had been his idea to invite Brady to the party.

"I HAD another idea about a change we might make," Jordan said as they walked along the beach. The sun was shining, sparkling on the waves as they raced toward the shore. The private beach wasn't empty, but most guests were sitting on wooden recliners or making the most of the cabanas, albeit fully clothed.

Brady wished it was warm enough to take off his shoes and feel the sand between his toes. "Hmm?"

Jordan snickered. "Maybe talking wasn't such a good idea out here. The ocean is proving to be too much of a distraction."

Brady whacked him on the arm. "I'm listening. You said something about change?"

"I thought we might move your desk into my office. If we're going to work together, that makes sense."

Brady smiled. "Let's wait until you've conducted the interviews, okay? That would be better." He let out a sigh. "Besides, I really don't want to think about work now, not when we have all this." He gestured to the ocean. "I have a better idea. Let's go back to the resort, order some hot chocolate, then sit by that fire pit we passed."

"Or we could sit on the couch in our room," Jordan suggested.

"That has certain advantages the beach does *not* have." Brady grinned. "Like the fact that clothing would be optional." He wasn't about to share the image in his head right then—Jordan standing naked in front of the window, his arms braced, while Brady was—

Jordan took his hand, did a one-eighty, and led him back to the resort.

It seemed Jordan wasn't the only one who had bright ideas.

"WHEN did you know?" Brady asked sleepily, his head on Jordan's chest, the soft sheets covering the swell of his ass. The temperature in their room was just right.

Jordan stroked up and down Brady's bare back in a languid motion. "Know what?"

"That you loved me?"

Jordan considered the question. "Maybe when we first arrived here on Friday. Up until then, I'd been attracted to you, but I think it was that moment when I first realized I wanted it to be real."

"Real?" Brady raised his head and peered at him.

Jordan stroked his fingers along Brady's jaw. "Not a pretend boyfriend." He shook his head. "All that trouble we went to, buying you new clothes so you'd feel comfortable here, so you'd look the part, and you know what? I just wanted to tell you that you're perfect whatever you wear. Because it wasn't what was on the outside that mattered. It was the man underneath who stole my heart."

Brady's breathing hitched. "That might be one of the sweetest things you've ever said to me. And just for the record?" Brady gazed into Jordan's eyes. "I wanted it to be real too."

Jordan tugged him until he straddled Jordan's waist. He pulled Brady down into a kiss, not really surprised when the air between them crackled with sexual electricity, and heat surged through him.

Making love to the sound of the ocean—a joyful, sensual experience that would be forever burned into his memory.

BRADY hadn't been remotely surprised when, after breakfast, Jordan expressed interest in going for a walk. It seemed neither of them was in any hurry to return to real life. He drove them to Lake Montauk, and they strolled along the shoreline, listening to the cries of the birds circling high above them, the waves lapping over rocks, or the soft chug of boat engines.

He'd never seen so many boats. Everywhere Brady looked, there were fishing vessels of all descriptions. He stared at the impressive yacht clubs and sailing clubs that were located around the lake. Jordan took his hand as they walked past Star Island, heading to the north of

Montauk. And when they finally left the water's edge and strolled along Soundview Drive, Brady enjoyed looking at the pretty homes along the waterfront. He and Jordan tried to put a price tag on some of them but gave up when they realized the starting price would have been at least a million dollars for each one.

"What would we do with four bedrooms and four bathrooms anyway?" Brady reasoned.

Jordan laughed. "Nothing, unless you've changed your mind about children."

Brady snickered. "That would be a no." They turned left to walk along a residential street, lined with the same immaculate houses, that—

He came to a dead stop, staring at one particular property, just visible above the treetops. "Jordan," he whispered.

Jordan came to a halt beside him. "What's wrong?"

"That house." There was nothing special about it. Its exterior walls were covered in a tired, sun-bleached pale wood, a two-story house with an upper balcony that ran along two sides, a wooden staircase descending from it. Yet Brady couldn't take his eyes off it.

"What about it?"

Brady pointed to the signpost at the edge of the street. "It's for sale, that's what." He grinned.

Jordan gaped at him. "That? It's a fixer-upper."

Brady nodded, still grinning. "All it needs is some TLC. But think about it. It's right by the water. By the ocean. It's perfect."

Jordan chuckled. "You must see something that I don't."

Brady got out his phone and tapped in the number of the realtor.

"Hey. What are you doing?"

"Getting some more details about the property." Brady had no clue why the house had made such an impression. He only knew he wanted to learn more about it. The house didn't have the same feel as the other swanky properties in the street. Maybe that was it.

It needs a makeover. The thought made him smile.

Then he realized his mind had gone off on a tangent. Brady returned his attention to his phone, but stopped when he heard Jordan speaking.

"Hi, is this Michael Darby? My name's Jordan Wolf. I'm interested in a property you have listed on Duryea Avenue, Montauk. … Yes, that's the one. What can you tell me about it?"

Brady stared at him, openmouthed, his phone still in his hand. When Jordan finished the call, Brady put his hands on his hips. "I'm not capable of talking to a real estate agent?"

Jordan smirked. "You got… distracted. I stepped in. So, do you want to know about the house or not?"

Brady rolled his eyes. "Duh."

Jordan counted off on his fingers. "Three beds, one bath, built in the seventies, with approval already granted for a pool." He pointed to the sandy lot in front of the house. "There, specifically. It has no AC, it needs renovating… and it's less than I thought it might be."

That last part filled Brady with hope. "Does that mean we could afford it?"

Jordan laughed. "Yes—*we* could afford it. If *we* so desired."

"So…?"

Jordan shook his head and sighed. He got on his phone again. "Mr. Darby? Hi. Jordan Wolf again. Do you think you might be able to show the property to myself and my partner this morning? … Perfect. … See you in half an hour. Thanks." He disconnected the call and peered at Brady. "Happy now?"

Brady launched himself into Jordan's arms. "Yes!" He kissed him exuberantly on the mouth.

Jordan started laughing. "Hey, don't go scaring the nice people around here who might end up being our neighbors."

Brady snorted. "Think of it as giving them a heads-up."

IN the back of the car, Brady leaned against Jordan, the lights of New York City speeding past, almost in a blur. By the time they'd reached Manhattan, rain had begun to fall, and the streaked car windows did little to lift his mood. Their idyllic weekend was finally at an end, and as they drew closer to Harlem, his heart sank further and further.

Jordan clasped his hand. "Nearly there."

"Sure." They were only a few blocks from his apartment.

"So, when we get there, I'm giving you ten minutes max to get in, grab what you need for tomorrow, then get out."

"Huh?"

Jordan smiled. "I thought you might like to stay with me tonight. Unless you really *do* want to go home and sleep in your own bed?"

Brady laughed. "You know, for an intelligent man, sometimes you say the dumbest things." He squeezed Jordan's fingers. "Of *course* I want to stay with you tonight. I want to stay for as many nights as you're willing to put up with me."

Jordan leaned over and kissed him. "In that case, we'd better organize a U-Haul for next weekend." The car came to a stop. "Remember. You have ten minutes. Because when we get back to my place—*our* place— we have a lot to talk about." He shook his head. "One minute we're going for a nice walk around a lake. The next, we're buying a house in Montauk."

Brady regarded him closely. "Regrets?"

Jordan kissed him again. "None whatsoever. Now move your ass." He leaned forward to ask the driver to pop the trunk.

Brady climbed out of the car, collected his bag, and sprinted up the steps to his front door, not bothered by the rain.

He was too busy thinking about his new life that was just beginning.

Epilogue

One year later

BRADY closed his desk drawer with a satisfied sigh.

Jordan snickered. "You are such a neat freak, you know."

Brady gave a gasp of mock hurt. "Just because *some* of us like to leave a desk neat and tidy." He glanced across at Jordan's, noting the piles of folders, and wagged his finger. "You're not going to leave it like that, are you?" He grinned, awaiting the backlash.

He didn't have to wait long.

Jordan glared at him. "Once. I let it get untidy *once* and you—"

The door opened and Kelly entered, her tablet in her hand. She narrowed her gaze. "Mr. Wolf, you should take a leaf out of Mr. Donovan's book. A cluttered desk is the sign of a cluttered mind."

"But I—" Jordan bit his lip, and Brady tried not to laugh. Then Jordan gave him a sideways look before muttering, "Then what is an empty desk a sign of?"

Brady fired him a warning glance before giving Kelly his full attention. "Now, you have all the notes for tomorrow and Monday, right?"

Kelly rolled her eyes. "You're only going to be out of the office for two days. I think we can cope. And yes, I've already emailed the heads of department, posted the schedules, and listed the meeting for when you get back." She grinned. "The company will still be in one piece when you return on Tuesday."

Brady blinked and stared at Jordan. "When I was your PA, was I this…."

"Efficient?" Kelly offered, her eyes wide.

"Not quite the word I had in mind," Brady muttered.

Jordan laughed. "It's a good thing Kelly is used to our little ways."

"She just likes poking me, don't you, Kelly?" Brady gave her a mock glare.

Kelly smiled sweetly. "Of course. How else do you expect me to get my shits and giggles?"

The fact that she felt comfortable speaking to them in such a way said a lot about their working relationship.

"And don't listen to him, Kelly," Jordan said soothingly. "*I* appreciate you."

She snorted. "Yeah, right. Only because I buy your favorite coffee and sneak in snacks for you when Mr. Donovan isn't looking." She covered her lips with her hand. "Oops."

Brady nodded slowly. "Snacks. *Now* I get it. Now it all makes sense. 'Kelly's a treasure, Brady.' 'She's a wonderful assistant, Brady,'" he mimicked before giving Jordan a hard stare. "Snacks?"

"My homemade vegan cookies," Kelly offered. "Healthy recipe, honest." Her perpetual smile faltered. "I wouldn't give Mr. Wolf anything that's bad for him." She huffed. "Now, please, you two. Get out of here, go home, and have a wonderful anniversary weekend."

Jordan gaped. "How did you know it's our anniversary?"

Kelly gave another superior eye-roll. "Duh." She pointed to Jordan's desk calendar, where the date had been circled in red, and the word *ANNIVERSARY!* written. Kelly's grin was back. "Gee, I wonder whatever gave me that idea." She turned and marched out of the room, humming to herself.

Brady chuckled. "I think the company is in safe hands. I thought *I* was organized until we took on Kelly." Of all the applicants for the position, she'd shone at the interview.

Jordan snickered. "Yes, but you didn't poke me as much as she does." Then he tilted his head. "Well, maybe less in the beginning. You got more pokes in later." His eyes twinkled.

Brady walked around the desk to where Jordan sat, hands outstretched menacingly. "If it's poking you want…."

Jordan launched himself out of his chair, laughing. "Grab your jacket and let's do as she says. We have four whole days together in our favorite place in all the world."

That brought an end to anything Brady might have had in mind. "Now you're talking."

Four days in Montauk. And the chance to celebrate their one-year anniversary in the place where their life as a couple began.

Bliss.

There was a knock at the door, and Kelly poked her head around it. "Do you have a moment before you leave?"

"Sure." Jordan slung his bag over his shoulder.

The door opened, and Brady stilled at the sight of four of the department heads, all smiling.

"We wanted to catch you both before you left." Dan Fremont held out a long bag to Brady. "This is from all of us. Just a little something to get your celebrations off to a good start."

Brady took it and peered inside. "Aw, champagne. Thank you, but you didn't have to do this!" He showed it to Jordan.

"It only seems fair," Dan commented. "When Celia and her husband celebrated their wedding anniversary last month, you two sent them some beautiful flowers and a great bottle of wine. We thought you deserved something similar." He smiled. "You make a good team." There were murmurs of approval from the others. "So enjoy your weekend, and we'll see you Tuesday morning."

"Unless we suddenly get a phone call to say you're staying a little longer," Kelly added, her eyes sparkling. "Which, frankly, wouldn't surprise me in the slightest, knowing you two."

Jordan's gaze met Brady's, and Brady could see the emotion he struggled to hide. "Thank you, all of you. We didn't expect this."

Brady nodded in agreement. "And we *will* be here Tuesday." He gave Kelly another mock glare, daring her to comment, but she merely gave him a sweet smile and ushered the staff from the office.

Once the door had closed behind them, Jordan took Brady in his arms. "It *has* been a good year, hasn't it?"

Brady had to admit, Jordan had been correct. No one had batted an eyelid at the change in circumstances. In fact, they'd received so many cards congratulating them that he'd been overwhelmed. And once he'd taken up his new position, the transition had gone without a single hiccup.

"Dan's right, you know. We do make a good team."

Jordan kissed him lightly on the mouth. "We always did."

Truth.

JORDAN closed the trunk and slung their bag over his shoulder. Brady was already climbing the stairs, two at a time. Jordan had to smile at his eagerness. Every chance they got, he and Brady would drive to the house that had become their safe haven. All of the renovations had been completed by the end of spring, and that had resulted in quite a few shopping trips for furniture and fittings. Jordan loved the peace and quiet of Montauk, but better than that were the opportunities to share quality time together, with none of the distractions of home.

By the time he reached the door, Brady had already set up the coffee machine and was busy putting away the groceries they'd bought on the way. That was their habit—to ensure the refrigerator and cabinets were

well-stocked so they didn't have to waste a moment
going shopping.

Jordan closed the door behind him, and suddenly
his arms were full of Brady, kissing him on the lips and
cheeks, arms locked around his neck.

"I thought today would never get here," Brady said
with a sigh. "I kept pulling out my phone and staring at
the photos of the house and the beach, wishing it was
Friday already."

Jordan chuckled. "Like I didn't notice. And I
wasn't the only one. Kelly would smirk every time
your phone came out."

Brady glanced around them. "Just think. It was a
year ago this weekend that we saw this place for the
first time."

Jordan chuckled. "Mm-hmm. A year since *you* saw
this place and got hit by a thunderbolt."

Brady laughed. "That *was* you on the phone,
wasn't it, calling for details? I don't recall having to
twist your arm." His nimble fingers found Jordan's ribs.
"Come on, confess. You loved it from the first moment
you saw inside it."

Jordan grabbed Brady's wrists. "Okay, okay, I
confess! Now stop with the tickling." He planted a kiss
on the end of Brady's nose. "So, what would you like to
do? The rest of the day is ours." Their alarm had gone off
at the crack of dawn, and they'd been out of Manhattan
before nine.

Brady grinned, took Jordan's hand, and led him
toward their bedroom.

It didn't take a genius to work out what activity
he had in mind. Not that it hadn't also been in Jordan's
mind too.

Thank God they were no longer buying shares in the condom companies.

"BRADY. Brady!"

He stirred beneath the sheet, then reached for Jordan, spooning around him. "Hmm?" Brady ran his hand over Jordan's hip, caressing it. "Why do you always feel so good in this bed?" It was always the same. At home, he was up with the dawn. By the ocean, he could spend hours in bed with Jordan, until they absolutely had to get up.

Jordan snickered. "I'd feel good to you in any bed. Or on the couch. On the rug. There was also that time on the kitchen ta—" He yelped when Brady tickled his ribs. "Hey! I was just saying. And I woke you up because you don't really want to lose the day, right? I thought we'd go for a walk on the beach after lunch."

Brady liked that idea.

"And…." Jordan rolled over. "We've just had a text from Belinda. She and Drake want us to meet them for a drink tonight, at Gurney's."

"Oh." As much as Brady loved seeing the couple, he wanted Jordan all to himself that weekend.

Jordan cupped his chin. "Think of it this way. It's only Friday. We go for a drink, and then we have the rest of the weekend to ourselves. We don't have to see another soul until we leave here Monday evening."

Brady could live with that. "I guess."

"And in case you've forgotten, it's their wedding anniversary too."

That changed things a little. It seemed the least they could do. After all, if it hadn't been for their party the previous year, Brady would probably still be suffering the effects of unrequited love.

I owe them a lot.

"Okay. I guess we can cope for a couple of hours."

Jordan frowned. "Cope with what?"

Brady grinned. "Withdrawal symptoms." Then he yowled when Jordan's hand landed with a crack on his bare ass. "Hey! No spanking."

"Aww. Not even anniversary spanks?"

Brady glared. "Only if you want to lose your fingers."

Jordan hastily removed his hand. "No thanks. I have plans for them later."

"Exactly." Brady threw back the sheets and climbed out of bed. "And I have use for them now. In the shower, Mr. Wolf." He padded across the floor to their newly added bathroom.

Whoever invented double showers was a genius.

JORDAN paid the taxi driver, then walked with Brady into the resort lounge, scanning the room. There were several empty couches and chairs, and no sign of Drake and Belinda.

"What time did she say they'd be here?" Brady asked.

"Seven thirty. Maybe they're outside on the terrace."

"Excuse me, sir?"

Jordan turned toward the speaker, a young man standing behind the bar, who smiled politely at them.

"Are you looking for Mrs. Daniels?"

Jordan nodded, and the young man gestured to their right. "Follow signs for Latitude, sir. They're waiting for you."

Jordan thanked him, and then they left the lounge. "Latitude?"

"Sounds like a suite or something," Brady commented. He pointed to a sign outside a closed door. "There."

Jordan pushed open the door—and froze at the sound of many loud voices yelling, "Surprise!"

"What the—?"

There had to be about thirty people in the room. A banner strung across the windows declared *Happy Anniversary, Jordan & Brady!* Belinda stood by the door, beaming, with Drake at her side. Behind her were several familiar faces, including—

"Mom? Dad?" Jordan gaped. Beside them were Fiona and Corbin, both grinning like idiots.

"Did you really think we'd miss out on seeing that look on your face?" Mom said with a grin. "Besides, it was high time we got to meet Brady's parents in the flesh, after so many phone calls between us."

Brady let out a gasp. "They're here?" Then he gave a soft cry when they appeared, enfolding him in a hug. "When did you get here?"

"We flew in this afternoon." Brady's dad grinned at Jordan. "We've had a great time chatting with your parents."

Belinda approached Jordan, holding out two champagne glasses. "You might want these."

"*You* are too sneaky for words," Jordan said, narrowing his gaze.

She glanced around the room, still grinning. "Well, I said I'd throw you a party. I just didn't mention that it was going to be a *surprise* party."

Jordan shook his head, chuckling. "What amazes me is how you managed it without anyone giving the game away." He fixed Fiona with a firm stare. "And yes, I mean you."

Fi opened her eyes in what was clearly intended to be an innocent expression. "I have no clue what you're talking about."

"Yeah, sure. And that Christmas when I bought Mom those earrings. You know, the ones she already knew about before she opened the box? I wonder how she managed that?"

Brady nudged him so violently that he almost spilled his champagne.

"What was that for?"

Brady leaned in close as he took his glass from Belinda. "Play nice, enjoy our party, drink some champagne, and talk to our guests."

Brady's dad laughed. "I see he's still bossy. No change there, then."

Jordan rolled his eyes. "You have *no* idea." He glanced at his own parents. "Should I be worried about the four of you getting together?"

Mom cleared her throat. "Don't you think it was about time? After all, you've only been living together an *entire year*."

Brady's mom giggled. "Well, I'm glad we finally got the opportunity. I've been wanting to meet you too." The two women began chatting animatedly, and their husbands exchanged glances.

"They've been like this all afternoon," Dad said with a smile. "You'd think they'd have run out of things to say by now, but no." He gestured to the server who was circulating, carrying a tray of champagne. "Another glass?"

"Great idea."

Brady slipped his hand into Jordan's as the two men found an empty table and sat down, already lost in conversation.

"Well, that's them taken care of for the rest of the evening. My mom could talk a glass eye to sleep."

Jordan almost snorted champagne through his nose. He gazed thoughtfully at their mothers. "What do you suppose they're talking about?"

Fiona snickered. "I'll lay even money they're discussing weddings. Well, one in particular." She grinned at Jordan and Brady, an evil glint in her eyes. "And I don't mean mine."

Brady groaned. "They wouldn't—would they?"

Jordan chuckled. "They can discuss it all they like. Doesn't mean it's going to happen any time soon." He took Brady's hand and kissed his fingers. "*Our* schedule, babe, not theirs."

Brady arched his eyebrows. "You *have* met my mom, right?"

Fiona and Corbin walked off, her shoulders shaking with laughter.

Jordan gazed across the room as a familiar figure raised a glass to them. He nudged Brady. "Look who else is here," he said, indicating her with a nod of his head.

Brady's eyes widened, and he dashed across to where Phil stood, laughing. It warmed Jordan's heart to see them hug. Brady had kept in touch with Phil since the move, and they occasionally went out for a meal or to a movie. Phil was the reason they'd ended up at a rescue shelter, choosing a kitty. Except when they'd gotten there, a pair of eight-week-old brothers had stolen their hearts, and they'd come home with not one kitty, but two.

Thank God Donna was willing to cat-sit all those weekends they spent at the beach house.

Belinda walked over to him. "So, are you still talking to me?"

"The jury's still out on that one," Jordan told her.

She sighed. "Honestly, when I first had the idea? It was going to be just drinks, just the four of us. Then it kind of... snowballed."

"Yeah, things always do where you're concerned." Jordan glanced at their guests. Some he recognized from the previous year's party, and realization struck. "This is for you too, isn't it?"

She gave a shrug. "Like I said—snowballed. Your parents loved the thought of surprising you, and they jumped at the idea of spending the night here. So I thought, what the hell, let's have a party!" She smiled as Brady walked toward them, grinning. "I take it inviting Phil was the right thing to do. Not that I had much to go on, only Brady's old address. It's amazing what you can find out during what seems like a random conversation, isn't it?" Her eyes gleamed.

Brady laughed and kissed her cheek. "You are a sneaky woman. Maybe the sneakiest. Yeah, definitely the sneakiest. Now all those coffee morning conversations at your place make sense."

"I just asked Jordan if he was still talking to me. I guess you are."

Brady gazed around the room. "Not exactly how we envisaged this evening going, but yeah, this is great."

Belinda gave them a sheepish smile. "About that. I know I sort of hijacked your night, but don't think you have to stay until the end. Why not spend a couple of hours, then sneak out?" Her eyes twinkled. "I'll make excuses for you." She grinned. "I'll tell them you were... tired."

Brady's snort rivaled Jordan's. "Yeah, I can see everyone believing *that* one." Brady's eyebrows almost disappeared into his hairline. "Tired?"

Belinda's lips twitched. "I think that would go down better than the truth." When Brady snickered, she rolled her eyes. "My God. You are such a kid."

"But you said—"

"Yes, I know what I said—and I also know what went through your grubby little mind." She shook her head. "You two were made for each other." Belinda walked away, still shaking her head.

Jordan put his arm around Brady's waist. "I think that's the nicest thing she could have said. And it *was* good of her to give us an out."

"Which we're not taking," Brady said quietly.

"We're not?"

He shook his head. "All these people are here to help us celebrate. I think the least we can do is stay until the end." Then he smiled. "They can go to their rooms, but I get to take you home. We'll have the rest of the weekend to celebrate together."

"And the rest of our lives to spend together," Jordan added, before kissing Brady on the lips.

Brady locked gazes with him and raised his glass. "I'll drink to that."

Coming in March 2018

Dreamspun Desires #77

A Model Escort by Amanda Meuwissen

What's the value of love?

Shy data scientist Owen Quinn is brilliant at predictive models but clueless at romance. Fortunately, a new career allows him to start over hundreds of miles from the ex he would rather forget. But the opportunity might go to waste since this isn't the kind of problem he knows how to solve. The truth is, he's terrible at making the first move and wishes a connection didn't have to revolve around sex.

Cal Mercer works for the Nick of Time Escort Service. He's picky about his clients and has never accepted a regular who is looking for companionship over sex—but can the right client change his mind? And can real feelings develop while money is changing hands? Owen and Cal might get to the root of their true feelings... if their pasts don't interfere.

Dreamspun Desires #78

Whiskey to Wine by BA Tortuga

Love is hitting slopes, and the competition is fierce.

It's Gay Ski Week in Aspen, and blind sculptor Bleu Bridey and his ex-fiancé, Dan, are at the Leaning N Ranch to unveil Bleu's latest commission.

Former Olympic snowboarder Ryan Shields is there too… and he's Bleu's true love who got away. Seeing Bleu again, Ryan remembers how they couldn't get enough of each other in college.

Too bad it looks like Bleu is with Dan now, because Ryan would love to remind Bleu how good they were together, in and out of the sheets.

Between Ski Week parties, a bunch of exes, a private ski lesson, and one terrible accident that leaves Bleu stranded and Ryan in rescue mode, it'll be a wonder if these two manage to survive, much less find a few seconds alone to remember how much love they have to keep them warm even in the worst of storms.

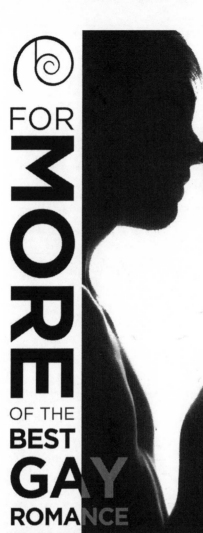